# Georgiana

# GEORGIANA

A NOVEL BY

*Maude Hutchins*

A NEW DIRECTIONS BOOK

Part One

*Chapter One*

*A*S A BOOK SHOULD
rest upon a table, as fruit in a basket, as a column, even Doric, on
a base, as a golfer takes his stance, as a battle has a field, as a radio
must be grounded, so I suppose the person I am going to tell
about should have a terrain, a place, a house, perhaps the house
should be upon a hill or in a valley or facing west giving her a
setting sun to remember; as a matter of fact, the latter thing is
true: she never, ever, all her life could place herself, on a train,
on a boat, in a strange city, without first closing her eyes and
imagining herself back where she grew up, the bronze light of
the setting sun in her eyes, her heart rather high on her left, and
her appendix (which she always kept for this purpose although

surgically she lost it in between) rather low on her right. In this way she found out where she was going, which was the port side of the boat, and which way she should turn when she came out of the theatre. It was the slow way, not instinct in her, but it was sure, attended, however, by minor accidents; she would bump her head in an upper berth in the black speed of night making a point of knowing for herself from her own experience that the train was going east and home when it seemed for some contrary reason to be going west, headed for danger and insecurity, and the word of a black porter must not be taken in these intellectual matters; and not only did the train appear to be going in the opposite direction from that which according to the timetable and the porter and no doubt the engineer if he could be reached and questioned, but by a trick of her imagination and a criss-cross tilt of her head, the train sped at a hundred miles an hour toward the Atlantic Ocean and the cold bottom of that sea, or sometimes the Pacific, as an alternative. It seems clear she had to do something and she always did: imagining herself back, standing in her own front yard while she bumped her head in the upper berth and pinched her right handed stomach and her left handed breast, until the train reversed itself as easy as that and went fast, straight ahead and dead east for home; on a liner in the middle of the world at sea she was even more conscious of that very metaphor "at sea," and nothing helped, not even the sun itself until it became her own sun, and it did not count unless she faced it and so she got run into by people who always went the same direction, counter clockwise, around the deck; but she had to know, as I said; and coming out of the theatre she could not bear to depend even upon a lover and they did not always get a taxi because the taxis got snapped up by other people less conscious of space but with keen dog-like senses of direction. And may I add here, keen and dog-like, meaning no lack of appreciation for dogs, as such, but people as dogs, in their ken-nels (called houses), and in their yards, called fields (of en-deavor); and this bitter aside I ask you not to identify with the child, girl, and woman I hope to describe but with the author who has so identified herself with the fictional character she has mentioned that as a more sophisticated, less innocent, moderately disillusioned and consequently somewhat resentful person, she may act as a foil, or at least as an invisible chaperone, duenna, or conscientious parent to the everlasting platonic child of these pages, whom he dare not advise for fear of changing something he loves and whom he intelligently recognizes as an individual and not a possession. The fact that as I write this last description of a good parent I must admit I learned it from my heroine who between, in womanhood, her first and second baby said in the presence of witnesses, "I know that I am not having a baby, I am having a person," will show the reader early in his judgment of her that space conscious rather than direction conscious as she was, her space was inhabited and real, more so than the arbitrary sign-posted estates of others, and that she was not entirely useless as a female citizen if only for those words if they should be remembered.

If she must have a house to be born in and while being born surrounded by the paraphernalia of that process, event, so unlike her; a school to be educated in with pilasters, electric lights, a motto and baths, although her memory of that school is not that of a building but of a sound, hyacinths that weren't there, different colored eyes without faces, cool feelings, mild disgust, wanting to go to the bathroom and intercostal neuralgia running through it all like a maze made of string, sporadically coming, knifelike, for no reason in the night, and going away under the warmth of a girl's hand beneath the small offending breast; I say, if she must have a house, and a school and later on lovers, a husband, the color of whose hair you want to see when she never saw it; if when she travels she must go to particular places named in Baedeker; eat in the restaurants and at the tables under which the reader remembers placing his own feet; it is I who will describe these things for your comfort and security, not for hers, and I shall not overdo it because none of these things is characteristic of her and this story is about her, not you, and I want it to be true, not necessarily in things but in essence, artistically right, so that you won't complain of not being able to see the forest for the trees and that you will love the forest even if you can't build a fire out of it or carve your love's initials on one of the trees about where they measure for sap, metaphorically enough.

It is true she was born in a house, not a hospital, which in its very lack of *objets d'amour* would have left her probably even more disengaged, less nostalgic, absent-minded than she was; neither was it a haphazard house, built today and gone tomorrow, its roof off with the first half a gale, made of plastics, or full-blown from the basement guts of Montgomery Ward. It was a house worthy to be born in with copper gutters that the birds built nests in and a copper roof to one side that in a heavy rain sounded like machine-gun fire and in the early dew of four A.M. like a long whispered story to be continued in our next. Not even to make the reader comfortable, however, will I put twin beds in this house. People had been born in the big canopied furniture of it for so many generations and died in them for as many that a handy *décor* might have been successive notches and chronological dates as cross reference to the big Bible down in grandpère's room. Here I must explain that the description implicit in "down in grandpère's room" comes spontaneously to me from that space of my heroine's which I have begun to tell you about and not from my own recollection. I know the house well and her grandfather's room was not "down," but "up" like any other grandfather's room in a decent thoroughbred house, not a bungalow or annex, and down simply means that she remembers grandpère as always coming up; up to see what she was "up to," up from something he was watching get ripe, up to get his flute, his cigars, a favorite wine (it was kept in the cellar!), to lock himself into a bathroom, to find a blueprint of a chicken house, to find her grandmother, to tell her aunt he could run his own affairs, to tell her as a child that he could still hear her whistling although he had told her to stop it. He was always coming up and her grandmother on the contrary, funnily enough, down. Down to dinner, down to get the jelly, down to the duck pond and as she always saw her grandfather coming up the stairs, she saw her grandmother coming down. It does not seem queer when we realize that space after all was her terrain and not a house with stairs that people went up and down just because of the direction they faced, and everyone, besides, who has ever lived very long in one place knows that for them downtown (if a village) and down and uptown (if a city) are places not directions, and especially is this so for people who live at a radius, to come to, or go to; it even becomes a little confusing to figure out whether they are coming or going except to those who are confused about simpler things.

If the house was elegant, secure, well grounded, hardly a shambling thing held together by hinges and locks, balanced by corners, and steadfast not alone by the speed of the earth's revolutions beneath it (more of its character and the imprint of the small heels of my heroine in its superstructure later), the big barn, out of all proportion to the Victorian house with its latter-day additions, corrective plumbing, porches and roofs, decorated inside like a cathedral by successive generations hoping for grace or in the house striving for comfortable adhesive personal views and not unbeautiful therefore, it or the cathedral, was Hellenic, Athenian, Greek as an acanthus leaf. If it had no egg-and-dart design, no columns, no metopes or indirect lighting, it was in itself, nevertheless, a place in its divine proportion and floor plan and inner space for well brought up Gods and Goddesses rather than for the horses this one barned in splendor; no Pegasuses either, just ruffians, irrational as the cold barnyard mares and fed on oats, not honey. The huge date hacked into one of its lunging, supporting beams marked the year 1630 but its architectural perfection, its unfunctional beauty, might have characterized the year 500 B.C. and in it might have been celebrated that famous feast described in the Symposium during which that Alcibiades might have said, "These are the things, my friends. . . ." And the successive layers of red paint, eroded and slapped on anew, peeling, etc., reminded one of that same color and texture, too, that a Pompeian wall painting has, whether it be of Sappho or of Cupid. Anachronisms besides the thoroughbreds (two full blooded grandams in horse parlance and genealogy make you eligible if you are a horse, for the quadruped's register and the dizzy, brilliant, accidental biography of a creature who neither thinks, chooses, or prays, but who has, in analogy, the blood of an aristocrat; and the doom and everlasting burial of a hack) were several, including the dogs whose only resemblance to the artistically rightful owners of this barn was their narrow hips and full-muscled thighs reminding us of Hellenic athletes on all fours, and their puppies whose folded mugs and drooping dewlaps, if photographed, might pass for portraits of that unfortunate Socrates whose sculptured face all of you have seen and wondered at, so unGreek it looks upon your schoolhouse wall, and whose mothers' (the puppies') bitches to you and me, to suggest another likeness, held the same social position in the dog world and bore the same relation to their dog spouses as Grecian women held in town and gown and in the minds and hearts of their husbands. And the male pups, the pick of the litter, too, I might add, loved and romped together all in good psychic faith, exactly as pleasantly as young Greeks, and only left off to suckle their Greek mama. There was also a row of ancient carriages besides the contemporary and useful lot of dump carts and farm wagons and a yellow buckboard that it was still stylish to use if you belonged to the old-enough guard and were chic enough to get away with it, and more especially if you could control the well-fed thoroughbred whose oats all went to her heels, it appeared, and her heels at you, protected as you were only by the brilliant toffee-colored wood of a carriage named in honor of just such a mare as this one, addle-headed, divinely beautiful, as crazy as a witch, and just as silly of you to hitch up to this frail two-wheeler as to put a witch on skis instead of on a good stout broomstick with a high wind behind and proper ceiling. There was a surrey

with four-inch fringe hanging from its cream-colored top; a
phaeton; a couple of black, dingy, angular jobs reminding one
of the remains of umbrellas, with doors to crush your fingers in
and lamps awry, the shafts pointing upward with no visible
support; a regular middle-class buggy, and a fine cutter, its up-
holstery still handsome, painted as if inlaid, and beside this
generous sleigh with a middle shaft to accommodate and separate
two plump mares, I imagine, a sweet, small two-seated cutter just
big enough for slender lovers; and meant to be hauled by a glossy
hack no doubt. In a corner, its shafts climbing up the wall and
one wheel almost off but its axle still thick with grease, lay unre-
laxed and awkward the sulky that grandpère raced at a terrifying
clip when he was younger, but not much younger at that because
the girl of these pages feared very much for her grandfather
when, in a leather apron and heavy glasses to keep the mud out
of his eyes, he grimly took the reins between his gnarled thumbs
and curled fingers, and the handsome pacer, a stallion, after a
fit of the fidgets, a hand-stand, a reach or two for the sky, an
all-over shake followed by deliberate, individual, unbelievably
well-placed quiverings of his seal-like skin, turned an ear back,
heard the good word, rolled the yellowish whites of his eyes,
and obeying the gentle but fiercely controlled leave of his frail
old master started off, mincing and dancing at first in excitement
and anger, for the hard straightaway kept in order (rather
expensive) just for this. Whether this almost daily adventure
was insisted on to exercise the animal, or to assure grandpère of
his still robust health and his position of master both at home and
among the neighbors, invisible as the latter were, or to show himself that he was not afraid, is not clear. But grandpère's stage
fright before the event, which amounted to such symptoms as
actual trembling, the constant lifting of things and putting them
down, lighting a cigar he could not finish, picking his nose, but
never going so far as to take a drink although it stood there
decantered at his elbow, and the horse's terror which seemed in
some way akin to the old man's, both appeared out of all propor-

tion to whatever reason there might be for doing it and nobody else could do anything until that half hour was over.

In another division of the divine barn was a great iron vat, circular and deep, into which poor simple rats sometimes fell and ever after until they nestled up and gently rolled to the bottom, raced, slipping in smaller and smaller circumference with bright eyes fixed on the center of the vat like skaters taught to eye the designated spot as they leaned on an outer and inner edge. No one except boy cousins, and they secretly with a language all their own, knew why and what-for this huge vat and what it had signified in the past. *Cannibals?*

Down a path to the left was the play house which I believe was called rustic in style. It was made of unfinished but slippery branches easy to climb upon; the floor was of deep sand brought from the seashore and the roof was as open as the sides. The blue-eyed boy cousins ate the sand by the handful and when it rained they sat in smooth and slippery puddles until they were hurriedly called for and taken home as leaden as bags of cement and just about as lovable. Also, up the broad side of this play house a younger cousin, easily, like a monkey reaching from side to side, pulling after him his hinder parts and feeling for support with his bare feet, climbed, to the openwork roof; he was the show-off cousin; when in a temper a killer; nearly always a bully; sentimental; lover of his mother; easily moved to tears by a hungry kitten that in another mood he would hamstring; susceptible to croup, smelling the halls up with his mother's preventive measures; a crybaby; a tattle-tale; a person who had to have his strawberries smashed, bashed, cooked to a ruinous stew because of all the cousins, he alone, like a little bastard, got a rash from fresh ones. The little girl I am writing more about later found his blue eyes and quivering lips repugnant and his quick devastating temper a fearful frightening thing, shameful when some other object caused it and terrifying when it happened to her. She escaped from him in his rages only because she could run faster; she flew; sometimes hid and then waited behind something, in something, close to a wall, behind an upright piano, until his activity, followed by fatigue, calmed him, made him a harmless playmate for the time being; wanting to play at getting married or with dolls. The author having left him on the roof might leave him there forever as he will play no obvious future role *vis à vis* our heroine excepting that her racing heart, fearful, anticipatory and apprehensive as it was for the rest of her life was surely accelerated by this small asthmatic wretch who was after her daily, sometimes with a can opener (a particularly fearsome, intricate, tortuous appearing instrument to her and which as she fled she saw in front of her forehead although it was approaching her from the rear); and who, observing that she was fearful of ammonia, its stinging smell seeming to attack her whole body from the inside, entering her nose violently against her will and spreading like stringy, cold, searching fingers through her warm insides making her feel like dying, as it did, an unwelcome miserable attention that in her maturity she might have likened to rape — observing I say, her shuddering fright, this lad, whom I shall leave on the roof if you say so, would steal a bottle of the horrid stuff from the cleaning closet and coming upon her suddenly with her dolls, knowing also her embarrassment of affection and daydreaming playfulness with them and so, *double entente*, you might say surprising her "in the river," like Caesar's men, naked; and giving her no time to recover from her shyness, backed her against the wall, the open bottle to her helpless nostrils; this, too, a kind of hideous rape, his knees pressed into her in his hateful, nasty little-boy pleasure. Shall I leave him on the roof? No longer the show-off cousin but the cry-baby cousin? His face swollen with crying? The children too frightened to run for help? His cries of "mama, mama," finally reaching the gardener who comes, his hands red with berry juice and with an upraised ladder and an accompanying snort rescues the tearful monster? As if he were one of the cats almost daily taken down from high trees in the same way? And then the tenseness gone, the rest of the children (except the girl) dance around the berry-stained gardener as he bounces the boy into the air to cheer him on the way to his mama and they shout "cry-baby, cry-baby" as he is delivered into her arms? She frightened by his bloody appearance which is nothing but strawberry juice and he unharmed except in his soul?

Another path which can only be described as arbitrary fetched you up at the boat house; the only floater, to give it its name, a fragile canoe and it unused in Georgiana's time; only the bottom curving up and away from its spinal cord could be seen by upturned children's faces in the single gable of the so-called boat house which hung over the small pond, one of a chain of five, fed by springs on the estate of Georgiana's grandfather. In this pond our little friend had come near drowning; with bread and butter hands she had depended on a rustic branch and, fingers slipping, had plunged in head first only to be rescued by whistlings from the big-house porch when the splash was heard, as if she were a dog, and quick to respond like a little actress she started imitating almost instinctively the dog paddle of her dog friends, chin up, and like them soon felt the ground under all fours and crept out, shaking herself, but not whining, unwilling to cry, ashamed, as if the elements had administered a scolding, well deserved; and wrapped in blankets, eating hot salty milk-toast, she did not think the silence solicitude but shame, as if she had done something in private not admissible in public, found out, too, but not mentioned, and as a silent punishment left to herself while the others, though surrounding her, talked of current events. These ponds, especially the one she had plunged into, because she had, and because it could be seen from her window, she remembered in all kinds of weather throughout her life. When they were slick and blue with ice grandpère did his edges magnificently, dressed arbitrarily and inadequately in his black suit with no overcoat, and on Sundays in his morning coat, his little white wedge-shaped beard anticipating, taking the turns with him, very nice, archaic. A pond for a barometer she later in her maturity very badly wanted and always imagined on calendars vignettes of grandpère attired for the month, but like Caesar, monkeying with the calendar, wearing what he chose; grown, she tried to persuade her husband to have his suits made buttoned high as in one of these vignettes, not conscious that she was trying to make a great big man into the little one who will harass and menace her through her childhood, girlhood, womanhood. Even before the sound of the rain on the copper roof she saw the smooth surface of the pond quiver like the skin of a horse; then tiny, innumerable, infinitesimal pinpricks showed that it was raining gently, a spring rain that began to move the short green grass as well and finally stream down the window pane, slowly, like tears, doubtfully going around impedimental dust and seeds on the glass. Twice a year these precious ponds were drained; the slim black water snakes hid in the grass, the shiny trout that had been stocked in them for grandpère's pleasure disappeared, and odds and ends: limp watercress, an old shoe, a barrelhoop, a milk bottle, rocks that had been thrown on the ice in winter by the cousins and village boys, somebody's whistle and a rosary would appear. All these things would be raked up off the sandy bottom and actually the pond in this state would be scrubbed spotless. The gulls from the nearby sea would come and watch, hovering overhead, talking about it; the dogs tried and did bury their gory bones therein only to lose the scent when the ponds filled up; the ducks complained and got unbelievably dirty in 36 hours and little groups of turtles waited patiently. The chief subject matter in the big house was the ponds and variations of their looks and behavior this year, last year and the year before. The cousins rolled up their pantaloons and waded knee deep in soft sand telling tales of quicksand and whole armies lost in it. Georgiana dreamed at night of falling into the waterless pond and as she fell, no longer safe but suddenly fearless in the sense of "What's the use," saying clearly the last part audibly as she awakened "Is that all?" and each time this happened it seemed an effort to find herself in bed again and it an imperative thing to get up, brush her teeth, and face a milky, tasteless egg for breakfast after such an important, climactic, sacrificial decision about life and death. It was not these dreams alone that made her unafraid to die in later life, there were other things as well, but it was a sub-early-conscious knowledge which made her sweetly and courageously precocious but not arrogant, on the contrary sympathetic, if a little contemptuous of others.

Returning to the Big House for a moment in this search for scenery necessary for Georgiana's livelihood in the reader's matter-of-fact imagination, refusing, as we take it he does, to accept her, unattached, platonic, without the implements, tools, ploughshares, flints, of successive materialistic industrialism, to place her historically, glibly, among the shifting but inevitable, inescapable scenic backdrop of her little time, ballet dancer though she may be and out the window, to continue this metaphor, like Massine in *Spectre de la Rose;* returning to the Big House, not the least educational part of it for Georgiana was the kitchen. Geographically it was Ireland; sympathetically, historically it belonged to St. Patrick, but like everything belonging to St. Patrick, it was torn by inner strife, and North and South were battlefields here as in the old country, the soft, warm talk and God-Save-Us parentheses of the Celtic ones interspersed and versus the colder, British, Protestant vocabulary of geographic difference, lasting late into the night and heightening the color in one cheek only to drain it from another, as if there were just enough blood to go around and no more, noticeable to the gentlefolk, and felt by the children as they wandered in and out in proportion to the sensibility of each and what each had been doing that was sinful recently causing him or her to "catch" the blush of Nora or Nelly as easy as an air-borne measle rash and momentarily take away his appetite for bread and butter and jam. Here, too, realism smacked one in the face sometimes, making one walk on tiptoe; things were glimpsed and stayed with one visually clear as daylight through the egg-shaped hole in grandpère's photographic darkroom, but without introduction intellectually, logically unarrived at and consequently static, picture postcards without continuousness or hyphen or connection in Georgiana's mind, nothing to do with her really, things she shouldn't have seen, confidential; a responsibility she had not asked for and was fearful of. Besides the things she was not supposed to see there was a certain camaraderie, display of feeling, vulgarity, quick temper, affectionate behavior, lack of restraint in this part of the house that made Georgiana jump when she was called by name from the front and arrive expecting to be questioned with a distinct feeling of disloyalty: part of the time to the kitchen and part of the time to the 'drawing room. She became an acute observer of kitchen and 'drawing room behavior; recognized antitheses, shades, colorations, differentiation of the species, as it were, *accent acute and grave*, noted innuendo between kitchen bravery and 'drawing room courage, the juxtaposition of heroism, heroics and bravado of both gentlefolk and servants, the former not including the children who were a law, it seemed, unto themselves, a kind of organized minority practicing selective anarchy; idealists and perfectionists in spite of a real naughtiness that ran like a series of sporadic reflexes through everything they did and thought. In her maturity Georgiana wondered what happened to children when they grew up; what became of their contempt for easy going adults who talked big and acted small, while they as children were speechless from necessity but critical, arrogant, positive, sure that they were harboring the Old Adam but marking time, waiting for power in order to be good. Georgiana observed without diplomacy, although that is what it resembled, but entered into, neither; she belonged to no party, neglected alternatives and recognized that the children were not a choice, either, nor a third party, but an hallucination. She entered into their games but gave herself very sparingly; she feared their savagery; disliked consequences which included the unjust punishment of all for the misdeeds of one which her grandfather practiced and from which she suffered out of all proportion because she would not tell. With bared legs, the children were lined up like chorus girls, and switched with a pliant green willow switch, cut in a kind of absent-minded innocence that appeared almost stupid, because it happened often and she never caught on, by Georgiana herself, as part of a sinister punishment. "Here," that small, white-haired, blue-eyed grandfather would say, "you are the quickest and cleverest, you run down and cut me a switch that I need, find me the nicest one, quick now, be off!" Georgiana felt the feathery willow leaves against her face, saw the patterned, sky-blue pond between the branches and happily chose a perfect switch, neatly cut it sideways as she had watched her grandparent do in pruning and grafting his fruit trees, wanted badly the slick, sweet pleasure of peeling it and feeling its moistness but refraining because he had not said for her to peel it. And then without being conscious of in-between happenings such as the return from the lake and that part of it, like summer lightning in a cloudless sky came the stinging, curling, shocking beating. In absolute fairness he switched them all alike; going down the line and returning, while the children hopped, wept, wrung their hands, each according to his style, character, health, blue-eyed or dark, and perhaps the loudest howl came from the guiltiest but that I am not prepared to say, children being unpredictable, irrational one moment, according to Hoyle at the next and always one up in guile on the grownup involved in a contest like this. Georgiana was silent as the welts appeared on her legs and burning tears to her eyes but she was just as silent on other occasions when she was guilty. So that all her silence seemed to signify was hatred, either of someone or something, resentment, bitter and deep, mixed with horror and shame, humiliation and disgust, physical and psychic; and she could only win by silence, complete control, no show of feeling in this orgy which she desired to escape from. Perhaps she felt that her silence punished her grandpère, cancelling her own. Her character, by the way, developed, because of this resistance, out of all proportion to its need in her later life so that if Quixote-like she tilted at windmills it was not as a romanticist but, in a way, to use up the energy she generated, not purposely to waste her character, but of necessity. She recognized, rightly or wrongly, her little grandfather in the persons of later antagonists and she fought them tooth and nail with her silence, her contempt. The grown-ups, well fed, and unobserving of phenomena of this sort praised her highly when she took great ladles of castor oil without the whine that accompanied like an obbligato some of the other children's armistice, when this, too, was a form of resistance, a hatred of these people, a refusal to break down, be licked, cry, show any feeling whatever that might harness her to an undesired and despised being. She learned never to throw up and when she was grown could face ether with a smile, thanks to grandpère. I should like to add here that concerning other punishments of the grandfather's vocabulary in such Georgiana had not yet read Dante or she might have recognized and even admired the Dantesque flair the old man had in the pattern of his punishments: when she disturbed him and also behaved in an unladylike manner by running up stairs or down instead of walking, he would force her by his presence, holding his watch, to run up and down the stairs for twenty minutes without rest as if she were a pony on a treadmill; when one of the cousins punched another cousin in the stomach, he was made, pale faced, to punch grandpère in the stomach and what a genuine licking he got in return! And the time (no fair because grandpère wore glasses) one spit in another's eye, and he had to aim at grandpère's with fine results when it was the old man's turn. Punishment by punishment then and "All Hope Abandon Ye Who Enter Here" as well. But if some of the other cousins whose healthy male badness was improved by this treatment in the sense that they got badder than ever as they grew up, learning as they did simply not to be caught, Georgiana on the contrary never learned to anticipate a shock because she lived a little offside in her own cosmos where she was good and a sudden realistic beating taught her absolutely nothing morally although I have described the character-building resistance it developed. She became aware of this resistance very early, as she became, in fact seemed to be born, aware; older, she underlined the words of Nietzsche, "Resistance — that is the distinction of the slave," but the word she noticed was "distinction" — accepting the slavery as she did in her early youth. Later on, rereading him, she saw her error but also her possibilities and desires, and reading further on she found his "thou Shalt is pleasanter than I will," a kind of schizophrenia unworthy of her who felt herself entitled to "escape the yoke" and eager to accept the responsibility of freedom, choice, oneness. She learned, too, to avoid scenes, even pleasant ones, interrupting as they did her daydreams, and she never entered into the games of the other children whole-heartedly because she found part of her heart plenty, more than enough; and too much fun was painful. When the cry, "Let's play getting married," arose Georgiana agreed only on condition that she could be the horse that drove the delirious couple away. She waited outside, stamping her feet, neighing, feeling like a horse, in some amazing way, mimic that she was, looking like a horse, foregoing the pleasures of matrimony that the other children enjoyed. These pleasures were always the same in design: marriage consisted, and how these children recognized the skeleton of it so clearly I don't know, of a religious ceremony with the horrid cousin we took off the roof as the indispensable minister, a couple of sets of cousins as brides and grooms (the weddings were always double because it avoided argument); followed by affectionate, savage, puppy-like cavortings on a big double bed (all four) and after the drive (with Georgiana prancing, settling down to a pleasant trot) which came after the cavortings, dialectically rather than chronologically following the ceremony, a kind of really pleasant companionship in which the couples sometimes for a whole week were inseparable pals, whispering, defending each other, stealing for each other, giving up this and that for each other, actually feeding each other and so on, domestic and tender, until it was over and it was time to be an Indian, De Soto, a train. Georgiana, as I said, was the horse at these times but she was not exactly continent at others: seeking perhaps to avoid such a close relationship as marriage, her affairs might be termed illicit, without ceremony, unbinding, polygamous. Whereas the others over a period of years always chose the same mate, serious and monogamous, Georgiana sustained an image, sought something or someone here and there, gave the impression oddly enough of fickleness, steadfast as she was. The fact that she was an orphan, brought up with cousins, aunts, great aunts, grandparents, and even her one sister blue-eyed, anglo-saxon, with only the hearsay much-beloved in her imagination father as dark-eyed as herself, and with a reputation as wicked as she felt her own to be making him twice loved, added, I feel sure, to her lack of attachment, at least for any length of time, to anyone. As all these places and things are forming this girl as if they were food and drink for her body's growth; all these stable smells, divine barns, lanky dog-attractions, leaping, pawing horses, waterless ponds, kitchen palaver and 'drawing room regulations; so the boy cousins are her future antagonists and lovers; the small, erect, blue-eyed, arrogant grandparent fights for possession as the prototype of her profoundest love against the hearsay picture but closer blood-bond and incestuous drive of her dead father; these little men will trouble her in the future differently incarnated but recognizable; frightening. Her early choices among the cousins appeared to be based on nothing but desire, her later ones on the early ones, resulting in a queer unhappy anger and antagonism, and with the choice before her of dark eyes and warm brown skin came a deeper love, safer, but it, too, doubtful, changing, searching, with only a faded photograph and a powerful magnetism to depend on, undependable, dangerous, heart-breaking, and as if that were not enough to keep her future lovers on their toes, an overwhelming infant recollection and attachment for a real brunette, a genuine one-hundred-percent negro Mammy from whose suffocating embrace and thrilling love she had literally been torn by blue-eyed unbelievers who thereafter tried to orient her unsuccessfully into their feudal nuclear system; to accept their constitution based on moderation and discretion, motivated as they were, pragmatic; no place, I am sure you will agree, for this dark stepchild, at least once removed from these kin, and if half of her was potentially blue-eyed, it was not her heart's half and served only to confuse and anger her. A fairly long sojourn with one of the nicer but still blue-eyed, fair-skinned cousins became so intimate, secret, swearing fidelity as they did on a testament as old as the meaning of the word, unknown to them but surely more than a coincidence, recollection, that to her precocious horror his sudden illness followed at once by death, relieved her of a bond that would surely have been bondage; of a remorse and shame founded on something she could not place, only erased as it seemed to be by death. The deadening influence of remorse, a near miss, she was spared, as she was also any binding shameful love with a later lover who resembled him just enough to horrify her when she loved him most, and save her for variables and differentiations. After the death of this cousin, his funeral like a conventional bouquet no one wanted to wear, Georgiana played by herself for a long time, in mourning, it seemed to others, for his loss, but really on a vacation, an exciting selfish respite, a deliberate forgetfulness pigeonholed for future reference, nevertheless, but temporarily a time for dreaming, a vacuum, like falling in the waterless lake during which, momentary as it seemed, and, oddly enough, she felt safe, secure for that second of unconsciousness in which she was not her own boss, need make no decisions, but "all right — I give up — how pleasant."

At about this time Valentina joined the household; a stranger straight from Bohemia, via the Statue of Liberty and the Pennsylvania Station, she walked into the kitchen with red cheeks, round calves and big eyes, and Georgiana remembered her coming and her going. She lent a kind of accent to the servants' quarters as if a red apple got mixed up with the potatoes. She was never really accepted by the Irish and only filled in, as it were, and never really belonged to the household. Georgiana and she exchanged glances, almost sympathetic, and Georgiana confused Bohemia with Utopia as something strange, a new world, a piece of jewelry. Valentina scrubbed floors and her dark hair fell over a cheerful face, and her plump pink knees slipped over the soapy surface she scrubbed quite happily. She also put away the silver and fitted the spoons together and the forks and the knives like a little girl playing games. "Look," she said, "spoons lie on their backs, but forks sideways with their knees up." Georgiana looked and blushed but she didn't know why; Valentina's short speeches always had an untranslatable but definite appeal, physical. It was the same year that Georgiana looked up one day at the school-room clock, noticed the date written in colored chalk across the schoolroom blackboard and with a queer skip of her heart saw and felt that a year had passed, the events having escaped her, and she not only different, the children bending over their geog-raphies and a thunderstorm going on outside. That night Valen-tina had a baby. This part is difficult: The author has picked up some information, some gossip, superstition about babies; Geor-giana had no such experience even in curiosity. She had not formulated, had no one intimately enough connected with her to ask, that question, famous, almost rhythmical, insistent, "Where do babies come from?" She liked babies, noticed them, patted their soft hair when she came upon them in the village, but felt for them only a make-believe affection, as if it were part of her own charm, a shy appraisal of herself. She had not at the time of Valentina's baby any curiosity about sex at all, she did not wonder what people were doing but was aware only of herself.

About now, at least by now, the reader, if he has not already formed in his mind a nostalgic or literary picture of our heroine, must be demanding one; a physical description is imperative at this point, something of the surroundings having been described, a child or woman must leave her shadow, her silhouette, besides her perfume and the feeling one has of missing someone who has gone away on a train and left her suitcase behind. The difficulty in describing Georgiana however is that the feeling of loss when Georgiana went away, left you, said goodnight, was more like having your leg cut off, your glasses taken away, or a dream lobster changed into rose-quartz, hardly satisfying your hunger, than the subject matter of *Information Please* taking a turn from Debussy to names of the presidents: nothing took her place, no synthetic or ersatz could fool the most unobserving of her acquaintances. The antagonistic coloring of this girl was of course more apparent in the sense of a definite negation, nighttime, twilight, absence of sunlight, to herself than to others. She felt, without knowing, the scientific truth of absence, the theological dogma of evil, of denial and privation. She did not walk in the sun but inbetween in a kind of after-the-day but before-the-moon, light, and in this more or less metaphorical weather she was most contained, happiest and lovely to look at. If her face did not shine of itself, certainly some moon, itself dependent on the sun, lovingly and generously sought out and shone upon this small oval symbol, its outline so clear and sure and its texture and brilliance so unsure, so wavering, so unobtainable, so shy, retiring, that others, too, when there was nothing else to do might say, "Does she exist or is this something potential, about to happen?" I do not mean by antagonistic, complementary. I mean that there was no complement at all but a definite, disciplined, psychic quarrel between the dark-eyed girl and the blue-eyed lot. She was aware from the beginning of the difference she represented and instead of using her pigmentation as a plus sign she correctly, at least in theological analogy, accepted it as a minus sign. She walked lightly like a dead relative on the other side of the line and the gold hair and pink cheeks of her cousins and her sister, the blue eyes of her grandparents gave her a feeling of unreality as to herself; that they were real and sure and that she was only a probation, something that walked in its sleep, something that would disappear in too much light or too much noise.

The baby, I need hardly add, was a complete surprise to everyone, especially Valentina. Valentina's first surprised yell which started everyone running somewhere lifted the glassware a half inch off the sideboard and the telephone tingled as after a stroke of lightning. The children, in their beds, lay quietly or sat up straight according to their dispositions; the blond sister said with authority, "It is time to pray," but Valentina's screams so frightened Georgiana that she could not speak or move until after a full hour of it she began to shake as the intensity of her feelings involuntarily allowed her this relaxation at last. Nothing, it seems to those who remember the event, happened chronologically. In an hour the birth of the baby had been accomplished. Georgiana never forgot the terror, the excuses which she did not at the time recognize as such, the shame, the punishment of that hour. Early next morning, but not so early that the children were not up, looking seedy, all of them, from a wakeful night, Valentina was on her way out. Georgiana always remembered the tear-stained face, even pinker from the exercise of producing the little stranger as if she had been playing tennis, and in contrast to its realistic, earthy, shameful, buxom parent the look of the pale, spectre-like baby who though only a few hours old appeared to brace itself in the arms of Valentina and to hold its little tennis ball of a head erect on a skimpy neck, much as if its progenitor might indeed have been as protoplasmic a ghost as Valentina's protestations and denials implied and Valentina herself have been really playing tennis. Georgiana often wondered without clarifying her questions to herself what the queer little baby was; she did not so much ask where it came from and how it got into the house without anyone knowing (she believed Valentina that she had never laid eyes on it before), as "what is it?" She never as years went by quite identified it with a real baby; she never *knew* the answer even in her maturity. No answer came to her and it was such a powerful negation that she never got over it; intellectually fatigued by her efforts she let it drop; returned to the therapy of the doll world. But the little thing's undesirability settled in her mind, nevertheless, and never imagining that it could grow up or change she apprehensively expected it to reappear on some threshold of her life, some doorway she was about to enter or even on a picnic when she was happy and spoil everything. The little apparition in its un-likeness to real babies, lovable ones, symbolized and simplified itself in Georgiana's mind like a transparent coin superimposed but not quite successfully upon an actual one, much the way objects behave in an oculist's mechanism when one definitely needs glasses, or the incomplete eclipse of the sun by the moon. If this incompleteness signified the design, gradually also by elim-ination and simplification the content: a scrawny, featherless, orphan bird, its head sticking out of its nest, remained; and this picture, this signal, tormented her forever, sustained as it was by curiosity (it had no other sustenance and it looked it); her mind having divested it of everything else not to tire itself, I think, or seeking to protect Georgiana against the horror of that night which is a more doubtful conclusion. In her grown-up life an ornament on a woman's hat would recall it as if a tiny search-light played upon it and her subsequent depression seemed un-called-for in the midst of sprightly gossip and she sustained her reputation for being moody and an unsatisfactory fourth at bridge. She herself wondered at her unexplained discomfort and wanted to kick at the furniture and sulk. The same memory, brilliant and visual, returned when, preparing for her first baby, her happiness and feeling of going to a party was spoiled, became a dismal abstract fear, when the doctor, a sentimental female, folding up her face, opened an obstetrical book and pointed to a glossy print, prenatal: the little apparition! I must say here that it seemed also that she came to identify herself with this startling but sad little spectre (also unsatisfactorily; also as in my meta-phor of the eclipse) and like its design she was the moon rather than the sun, she walked in the shadow rather than the light and like its content she might be unloved but nevertheless spectacu-lar, the center of all eyes; different. But none of this was any clearer to the child than it is to the author, and no doubt to the reader, it only appearing fairly certain that the symbol became an object of fear and it reappeared at intervals all her life when other things seemed to be, and sometimes were, frightening her. (I am sure if I may inject myself here that everyone has a fear-symbol which is brought back sometimes by something resembling it [like the ornament on the woman's hat], and sometimes by a new and real fear. The author's private, ridiculous terrifying fear-symbol for which he must apologize, is a rabbit, not Freudian but Peter, part explanation of which is that for some reason not clear to him he identified himself with that Peter, who, himself lovable but naughty, experienced his own terror in his fear of sneezing in the watering can bringing down upon himself the holocaust of Mr. McGregor and his infinite ilk, over whom the obstinate, willful little Peter Rabbits have no control. I believe that the author's rabbit resembles Georgiana's featherless bird in its orphan-like quality, its ability to get into trouble and its fear of attracting attention by the inevitable sneeze and following furor, in spite of its desperate love of peace which its spectacular talents will not allow it, however.) After the maternal group *sorti* of Valentina, the children, as usual after a storm which seemed indeed elemental and which in this case they could not understand in varying degrees, from a know-it-all look on the sophisticated sister down to complete incomprehension by Georgiana, mated up and wandered off probably doing things they shouldn't in the intuitive simulation of that which had occurred but which they did not understand. Some of them remained in the woods or the playhouse or in the barns all day and grownups were relieved that all those, some bright and some moody, but all questioning, little faces did not have to be considered at luncheon. By supper time things had resumed their natural course, and events which had taken so long to reach a climax, seemed to be miraculously over and put aside. Valentina had sinned not only against God but against the New Englanders in this house and her ousting and immediate dismissal without any representation whatever was just; not a soul in the grownup world felt sorry for Valentina and in the children's hemisphere there was not so much regret for Valentina as a feeling of some sort of guilty knowledge of her deed or in some cases actual belief that one of them was responsible, that prevailed.

Chapter Two

IT WAS AS IF, at Valentina's dishonorable departure, a whole generation had been wiped out. That buxom "Renoir" who had been too cheerful to be good, too contented to accept the ancient Republican Manifesto of this rotting Victorian house had been, for the short time that is allotted youth itself, the allegory of youth with flowers in its bosom, in Georgiana's innocent microcosm. Old people and children remained; not only as if a war had called away all the young ones but as if those who remained were garrisoned as well. Society had long since quit laying its cards underneath a door behind which a proud and testy dictator with cold blue eyes had observed their pretensions, peculiarities, their lack of ancestry; and had sneered at the source of their incomes. His own income perilously reduced by taxes and no earnings; by unwise, even absurd investments into which he was persuaded by the unscrupulous and by his own cocksureness, arrogance and economic innocence; he despised the wealth of those neighbors who were in business or in trade and he refused the timid invitations of those few of the old guard lot who still lived comfortably on a combination of wisdom, credit and home-grown strawberries. He would not accept that which he could not return and he included his entire family, even babies, in this social dogma. Silver spoons for newly harbored orphans such as Georgiana and her sister had been and for nieces and nephews from various sources, arriving, it appeared for a while, on every other train, were returned to chagrined neighbors, and invitations to take a cousin or two into town to see *Peter Pan* were refused. The village children two miles away could not be considered playmates. Georgiana, then, lived with grandparents, great aunts, domiciled and visiting, and a batch of old servants who had no callers, the old man's pride and regulations including the kitchen. Grandpère was patriarch; there was not a male relative on the place; what killed them off I cannot say; one of whom the children vaguely heard, the husband of the aunt who was mother of the bratcousin of rooffame, was either not received by grandpère due to some minor sin, financial indiscretion; or himself refused to enter the house of the tyrant. It mostly depended on which end of Ireland was discussing the matter within hearing. For a long time letters came every day, pleading for reinstatement (the south of Ireland said) but the security, evidently, of the old man's autocracy superseded that of bureaucracy and the aunt stayed on, missing something badly but not badly enough, and Georgiana felt the thin shadow of this mildly discontented, rather neurotic, aunthood. She wondered at the apathy which neglected the call of romance, no matter how faded, dehydrated as a flower between the pages of an old book, but a flower, wasn't it? It also appeared that the old man didn't like men around his women folk, especially their husbands. He willingly housed all his returning daughters; in cold terror, felt by all, began to dip into his principal to do it and "ought to cut a notch in his gun" was figuratively suggested by an Irish wit, as each returned to him with her children or sent the children on to him, never to be heard of again, themselves, it seemed. One aunt remained in Georgiana's time, the one I have spoken of, but she was as old as far as the children were concerned as the rest; age had come upon her rather suddenly: after the death of her eldest boy, that same dear cousin, too soon angeled, with whom Georgiana had lived for a whole year in sin, the aunt had terribly shocked both the servants and the old gentlefolk in the house by an attack of hysterics. This expression of feeling so out of accord with all tradition in this house, so startling and shocking, had not gone unpunished, and the aunt had been banished somewhere for a whole year in order to pull herself together and act like a lady. The wild laughter of the aunt and the screams of Valentina had reverberated along the walls for a long time in Georgiana's imagination and in her dreams and she was certainly afraid. Some time later the falsetto shrieks of a female turkey scared by a horse reminded her of both aunt and maid. The aunt had returned chastened and silent and had become as old and as lady-like as was expected of her, the boy never mentioned again, buried twice, as it were.

And just as the children had no playmates, neither had the aunt; briefly and timidly the question of the D.A.R. came up; also, just as briefly and timidly, the Colonial Dames. Grandpère wouldn't allow either of these diversions, for two reasons: the hardware merchant's wife belonged to the D.A.R., the grocer's to the Colonial Dames. Grandpère was not a snob, his ancestry made that impossible by definition; neither was he a scholar although it was he who had pointed out to Georgiana that the word "snob" was derived from the "s. nob." found in old Cambridge records after the names of boys without nobility: *sine nobilitate*, "s. nob." Neither was he without respect for a revolutionary sword, signed by the first silversmith in America John Burt which he lovingly fondled. But grandpère was besides a Tory and had in his bureau drawer a bullet that had lodged in the Tory doorway of his ancestors while they were eating things common soldiers only dreamed of (Georgiana imagined these exclusive ghosts), and if he fondled the sword that was wielded by the wrong side he fondled it for its beauty rather than its deeds. Grandpère just could not imagine his daughter embarrassing the daughters of tradespeople by her presence at their games and did not think such a sorority practicable or conservative.

As I have said, the servants, too, had skipped a generation and a black coachman who was so old that his duties were negligible, even in this Yankee regime, hung around with nothing much else to do but respect the great aunts:

"Mornin, Miss Carelin."

"Evenin, Miss Sayrah."

Thus maidened as well as widowed, the aunts, a certain number of times a day, were girls again, in the memory, at least, of a senile Negro, who also remembered better times, gayer, and softer, gentler kinship with the southern gentlefolk before Mr. Lincoln had freed him, antagonizing so this family that in a desperate Freudian effort, I suppose, to forget the psychic pain of civil hatred they had torn each other from each other's hearts and memories, picture frames and old Bible genealogies: (the children found thick black lines and splattered blots of ink where the names of southern kin had been, savagely denied relationship by grandpère; just as that little old Hamlet, grandpère had inked out of his soliloquy his rival, that son-in-law; symbolically murdered him with the scrape of a pen: silence) so that now nothing passed between them; not even births, graduations and funerals were announced, so successfully escaped from each other they had become; and the Mason and Dixon line became a high thick wall that no cousin-lover could scale, or else the relatives, like chickens, refused to pass the designated thing even in thought. Only our heroine was left, in memory of a

handsome Virginian father, to feel almost a blood relationship
to an old darky with lavender skin and milky blue-black catar-
acted eyes whose whites were ochre-colored like a sick horse.
From this old man who bore her family name, refusing to change
it, despite grandpère, to fit New England pedigree, she tried to
find out about her Mammy and thus reconstruct her past which
she felt was a mystery, but the Negro told older tales than that;
mixed up her Mammy with her great-grandmother; only once
in a while reaching the surface with, "Oh, dat colored girl; she
trash. You donne know *her*, Missy. Phoo!" And so this only link
with her extreme childhood, which she wanted so to recall and
live over again, was useless to her as if some anesthesia had
blotted out everything after 1900 for him including even this
morning, and while Georgiana knew that her Mammy had been
old, he remembered her, when at all, only as an adolescent,
bawdy pickaninny, a crazy beginning enough for an old black
woman, without the two images superimposing themselves in
Georgiana's mind, confusing and frustrating her; in the end
reverting to the same feeling, sensation, rather than memory or
knowledge of a dark overpowering love, a fearful personality,
the subject, but undefined, of repeated nightmares which could
not be accounted for by too many covers or impending showers
with change of wind, suggestive as these barometric changes are.
She was too shy, too intimately connected with her father's
memory to ask about him and she also had a delicate inbred sense
which did not let her ask an old Negro about a white gentleman,
close as she felt to these people. But the lanky old fellow, stimu-
lated by strong hot tea on a summer day, told the children,
slapping his thigh, raising the dust, and laughing immoderately,
"Hyar, Hyar, Hyar!" about "that young master Willie." "You
chillen know what he do? Does you? Donne you tell um I tole
you! Heah me? Ah kill you!" and he would make a hideous, ridiculous grimace before settling down with a change of tone, gentle
and loving, to tales of the cute disobediences and saucy wit and
impudence of Master Willie, whom Georgiana knew to be her

father, but whose small boy's silhouette neither could she synchronize with the beautiful father of her imagination, any more than she was able to integrate the two Mammies, pickaninny and old woman of hearsay; of whom, the New Englanders had it, not only had she bewitched Georgiana, teaching her to have nothing to do with anyone but herself but that she had left with more than she had come, what's more, the figures, to be exact four to one, as in a Martini, leaving, they said, with four barrels, having come up from the South with one, and that not bulging, either. This line drawing of an old woman bending over a barrel stayed with Georgiana also, but it was merely intellectual, two-dimensional: her real recollection of Mammy was fearful, overpowering as I have said, as of a coming storm, not enough air, passion, south-wind, extra heart beats in the night, something she could not account for. Her queer contented feeling when she was with colored people at later times in her life seemed to give the lie to her fears which also stayed with her but not in their presence. There had been a period when referring to the olive of her skin so unlike theirs the cousins had called her, "Nigger," and the grandfather's fury had given her sudden cause to think "Could it be true! I drank black milk, didn't I!" and she was terrified at the thought of blackness, more orphaned than ever, balanced insecurely over a dark abyss. And a queer shock, too, to a little Virginian whose small white ancestors had had their shoes put on by black children; playmates and slaves, twins but not twins, separated socially by a must as powerful as a chemical. A few days after the incident the aunt had brought home presents from the village for the children. The center of all eyes as she unwrapped hers, slowly savoring what it would be, it came into view: a crazy, colored minstrel on a string. Georgiana blushed deeply but no color appeared, it never did, she alone felt it, followed at once by pallor. "He can jig — Georgiana can jig, too. I saw her when she didn't know it!" It was true she could jig and sometimes when she felt happy, suddenly free, without responsibility, she did jig. But she didn't jig any more.

No one knew about her fear and she gradually forgot it, but for a whole year she intermittently thought she was black, accompanied by genuine horror and no sympathy for herself at all, as there is, I am told, as well as a romantic feeling of superiority, in children who get notions of adoption and that sort of thing, the love of superiority in difference. Her cozy feeling, then, for dark and savage peoples began very early to accept, but not quite, the almost chemical censorship of social negation. The white race in her, bleached in the bluing of Anglican-Virginian aristocracy despised, affectionately loved, the black slaves at one and the same time; the economical New England blood fearing, more logically and with reason, the prolific coloration of the Negro. The lack of Q.E.D. is what disturbed her, and intellectually liberal as she was, she hated intolerance but accepted because it appeared she must, ambivalence.

Grandpère occasionally kept things in order, not because he could afford it, but because his father had taught him to, and grandpère suffered very much from the teachings of that papa which could not be integrated either: "Keep your house in order" and "Don't spend your principal." But not very much in sympathy with grandpère's moral problems, this is to introduce, because we are interested in Georgiana's, Mister Moon. Mister Moon was an expert carpenter and house painter; he was black by inheritance more than in coloration; he had that shade which is neither here nor there, a warm theatrical pallor which changed when he went in and out of the house from golden in the sun to orchid in the shadow. His features he inherited dishonestly, and he held his mouth, unlike his black Mammy's and great aunt's, in a horizontal superior kind of determined pain, forbearing his black jigging blood and moving quietly, with dignity, like a dirge played on an organ, maybe Bach, and polite to a point, but a very good, even expert, workman, as I have said. Georgiana came into the room he was painting in the middle of a daydream and in her hurry to step back out of it upon seeing Mister Moon, placed her wide open palm like a starfish onto the fresh and sticky, lukewarm paint of Mister Moon's talented profession. Mister Moon stepped forward; spoke to her gently as if she were a small wild animal caught in a trap, and wrapping his long fingers around her wrist, dislodged, almost without spoiling the newly painted woodwork, her brown little hand; she noted at this point that her hand, sticking out, widespread, as he held her wrist, was a shade darker than his and she felt the cushioned ends of his fingers digging into her wrist bringing out her pulse as if he were a doctor. In his other hand he held a clean rag as if he had been prepared for just such a despoiling as this of his art and its attendant painted palm to be cared for, and dipping the rag in a nearby tin of pungent turpentine, which raced up Georgiana's nostrils into her eyes as she bent over her own palm and his, he gently, firmly smoothed and wiped off the sticky paint, holding the back of her hand, now, in his and saying words she never remembered, so much more penetrating was the smell of paint and the feeling of his hands, warm, damp, clinging, exciting, lovely. She learned from Mister Moon, then, to recall the pleasure of dark skin, that pleasure that must have been hers even earlier than this, and critical, quick to make comparisons, she appreciated and noted the difference between this skin and that of the fair-skinned ones like her cousins, the latter giving off sparks, it is true, but dry, feverish, even squeaky when it was clean, while this skin was so soft, so appealing, so desirable, memorable, like one's own. And later, by herself, she felt her own palms to be sure and, it was true, the soft mounds at the base of each finger destined to give pleasure to others, were something special like small loving breasts on a boy; the palm was rosy-pink in its response, the first time any color, to speak of, had reached the surface of her skin; she sniffed the palm and it smelled delicately of turpentine. But Georgiana immediately censored her delight in Mister Moon's touch and hid it away, daring not look at it and avoiding Mister Moon at all times so successfully and with such integrity that she never saw him again. The well-remembered touch of his hands, however, she would know again in another and then another but not recognizing it as such, loving it, desiring it, but not quite.

38 How different was the appeal, appealing as they were, of the gypsies to Georgiana. Grandpère's strained lack of hospitality did not include gypsies, tramps, ministers of the Gospel, and those odds and ends of the social strata, flotsam and jetsam, that lunatic fringe which could not be pigeonholed; those irregular and defective verbs, as it were, those dangling participles, who, as a matter of fact, he housed and fed as part of his aristocracy which was so far removed from these queer ornaments of society that they did not concern him enough to be denied. In this relaxed, caesural-pause kind of state grandpère almost liked gypsies, tutors, tramps. They took advantage of this in many ways: a large white-washed "X" on the entrance gate was the signal for passing nomads (tramps who must not be confused with gypsies), that here was food, a dime, etc., a cup of coffee and no fear of being set on by dogs or buckshot in one's heels. Much to the justifiable annoyance, which grandpère coolly ignored, of neighboring country gentlemen, the annual caravan of gypsies, counterclockwise in their travels, going always East to West, not to a place but a direction, was welcomed, on condition that they camp on either of the two orchards furthest from his own house, and here they settled for a week or two in the fall, enhancing the landscape, Georgiana thought, with their bright protective coloration among the autumn leaves and adding something more in keeping with her daydreams, less worldly than her scanty surroundings. Platonic, abstract but still real, touchable, untouchable though they in orthodox considered themselves, and appealing to her imagination like a bonfire, they seemed to her pictorial rather than artistic, but their short stay lasted in her imagination throughout the year, using them up, as it were, one at a time, in her thoughts, as if they were hickory nuts put away by a squirrel. Descendants of an outcast, banished from the society of others, this fault or sin, this traveling expiation for an act of apostasy, became their pride, legend, and inheritance,

and these gypsies held their heads high and were afraid of no one, having been promised immunity, so they said; and they waved ancient scrawls of "safe conduct" in the faces of those servants of neighbors who had instructions to drive them off. Good-humored but malicious, swarthy, covered, it seemed, with penalties, inflictions like scars, with gold coins in his ears and smoking an Havana from a gold case their head man, calling himself a count, paid his respects each year to grandpère who received him outside, alone. But from her window Georgiana saw this strange pair looking even more anachronistic than in her later years the pictures of vice-presidents and Indian chiefs just before an election did, and she wondered about grandpère and his dogmas, principles, unconditional surrender, his unexplained regulations and no-quarter rule, his Dantesque punishments, his sentimental sprees, tears, anger, fury, passions, and what connection, if any, he had with grandmère, that silent old lady (could she possibly have had a night life?) whom he kissed under the mistletoe at Christmas and gave small but rare uncut gems in cushioned boxes covered with plum-colored velvet on her birthday. The gypsies, while they were domiciled in grandpère's orchards, became almost entirely the subject matter of Georgiana's daydreams, so much so that after they had gone she did not know which had been daydream and which real. If she had been communicative, which she was not, she might have been called a liar, which she was not, if she had retold the tales that she could tell. The attraction of the gypsies had been, as I have said, imaginative, pictorial, sexless, and as the only evil and therefore guilt that a child knows is that which is, in various guises, sex — am I right? — Georgiana had been free, uninhibited in the daydreams she had had concerning gypsies, and had not deliberately censored any of it. Even their persuasive kidnapping and her subsequent marriage with the head man and count was pictorial rather than sensational and at least consciously she was not aware of any sexual impulse. Her continued consciousness was more like a rogue story, picaresque, appealing to the adventurous, than a substitute of any more obvious kind. It was, as a matter of fact, an objective tale with Georgiana looking on, an epic without psychological implications, rather than the subjective, libidinous wanderings which she would later on know as well but not yet and not quite. Of the behavior and morals of gypsies themselves, the old Negro had this to say: "Dey donne *steal*, honey, dey just hep demselves fum de Lord's good ole bounty. You tink dat hay blong to ole marse? You think he *make* dat hay? Go long, you crazy chile, dat what, jus crazy like everbody."

And so Georgiana's life, inner and outer, had its colorations, its change of levels, its static and its moving pictures. She felt that she was standing absolutely still, all by herself, looking out of a window. It was only much later in nostalgia, that she saw herself in each picture as part of it and felt a real affection for the child, her only real child, her legitimate ones were, after all, persons and not hers at all. The relations I have introduced, the old people, servants, colored coachman, gypsies and more if you like: the village idiot, family doctor, surveyors, hangers-on, are, as I have meant them to be, a backdrop for Georgiana, unable, as we find, as she is, to exist by herself without them. At this time she appears as premiere ballerina supported by the dancers and much later this metaphor will still hold good, but only Georgiana will remain the same, the dancers have changed their identity but not their influence, and Georgiana pirouettes up to each and recognizes her old loves at last, but not before the strange anxiety of her movements betrays that she is lost, ill at ease with memory; this amnesia making her fall into the arms of strangers in her search for her early loves whom she does not know she is looking for. The only thing the author cannot explain about this figurative ballet is the coincidence: all her new loves are her old loves, and the distressing finale: her unhappiness at having found them. But perhaps more will become clear as more is told of her childhood and her maturity separated by that inbetween period, of adolescence, from which I shall quote only for the record, as it were, but which is of no consequence, seeming to serve in life as a period of sleep, a long nap, from which one finally awakens and begins the inevitable search of which I have spoken. At the risk of one too many metaphors one might liken this childhood — adolescence — maturity — to a receipt for cooking stringbeans: Take fresh beans; blanch (blanching is a process of scalding in large amount of water or quick cooking, parboiling); drain, set aside and cool; just before serving cook in small amount of water quickly and season. The result of this method is that the original color of the beans is set in the first quick cooking. The inbetween setting-aside of the beans serves only, it seems, to let it set more and the final cooking is much like the first. In adolescence, then, in this setting-aside period in which the color of one's childhood takes, things happen, it is true, and one behaves, but it is neither logical nor rational; it is a make-believe period in which one does things which would be odd if the period itself were not still odder, and it gives one time to set, a biological rest, hibernation.

# Chapter Three

*G*RANDPÈRE WAS
not mad but he was singular; peculiar in the sense of one of a
kind, an original. He was also a connoisseur, a gourmet, a perfectionist, a dictator, a frail blue-eyed monster. He had a sinister
patience, a terrible temper, perfect pitch; he despised young men,
drunkards, liars, laziness. He had no sympathy for weakness,
and included any expression of any kind of feeling whatever
whether one was gay or sad in this must-not. Temper, however,
because he had one, too, if not encouraged was not absolutely
forbidden; it appeared inevitable, almost elemental in this house
and the worst of all possible tempers was grandpère's. Other
people's anger seemed like minor tantrums in comparison with

grandpère's towering, one hundred percent rage when the stars were right and everyone feared the old man. Georgiana, young as she was without experience in pity, nevertheless pitied as well as feared him at these times and did her best to hide, run away, not look. Georgiana often did not know why she had at a given moment inspired his anger and sometimes looked around and behind her, to see if it could not be someone else that he meant. If the door was behind him she was cornered, trapped, and backing up against the wall, or taking if you can call it a stand behind a chair, stood her ground till it had passed. The horror of seeing the head man, the one whom everyone turned to, in spite of his lack of stature and appeal, at all times, frightened so badly this child, this incipient responsible one, that she scarcely dared breathe until he had regained the tiller, as it were, canceling the need for one to take over oneself. But grandpère felt fine following his fits of temper and so did everyone else. She always remembered his appetite after a scene, his good-natured, "This beef is cooked right for once," at table and grandmère's almost holy look of relief. Herself weeping in her relaxation after the event, she did not understand the oft repeated sentences she sobbed out, "He does not love me. He does not love me," because she was not in the least aware that she wanted his love, and she hated him. Always fair, however, she unreservedly admired his talents; he was a fine amateur musician, amateur draftsman, architect, amateur gardener, gentleman farmer, fisherman of parts. And she loved the things he loved all the rest of her life. Her impatience with other men when they could not do the things that grandpère did so well was well known. Grandpère taught her by emulation, induced by a mixture of scorn, punishment and real physical grace to build a proper fire, whittle, hang a picture, mend things, fix up the plumbing, plane the windows when they stuck, harness a horse, hold a live lobster or crab, bait a hook, tie a bowline on a bight, calm an excited animal, horse or dog, recognize a gentle one, splice a rope, wind a clock, fix it when it stopped, sharpen a pencil correctly, take the top off an egg in one neat swipe, get in and out of a screen door without slamming it when your hands are full, graft twigs, how to set a peach tree, where, which side of the wall to plant asparagus roots, a preference for wild strawberries, how to harvest things and when, how to lead a horse: obliquely (never, of course, face him), how to catch a bass (give him his nose), a trout (don't), a bluefish (ditto), a weakfish (wait), pick watercress out of the lake without upsetting, always leave the bloom on blueberries, never wash an egg; if (1) a bulldog, (2) a snapping turtle, (3) a squirrel gets a grip on you, wait, he'll let go if you relax. She admired this kind of handy folklore even more than his greater talents and no other man satisfied her love of this handiness, this neat, graceful kind of know-how, with no lost motion, no need to be strong, mind-over-matter kind of charm. She was the only one grandpère trusted with his knife, his flute, his newspaper (she, alone, was allowed to see it before him if she chose because due to his teaching no one could tell that it had been unfolded when she had finished with it), his camera, his tobacco, his julep (although she made and delivered it to him no finger print was ever found on its shimmering glaze). He even taught her to make a bed as it should be made, and she could turn out a salad at the table while the others less interested in perfection, merely hungry, but daring not show impatience, waited. The pallid faces of squeamish blue-eyed boys (beardless and lily-livered) did not inhibit grandpère's stubborn preference for a properly cooked duck (hardly cooked at all): the blood must run; if only the boys could have! Georgiana forgot her first repugnance, so cumulatively and successfully controlled that she, too, preferred a scarlet fowl to the soggy average of duck artificially flavored with applesauce. Grandpère's chafing-dish rabbits were divine and so were hers; the smell of simmering beer and the smooth look of shining cheese she never forgot; but all this appreciation was for her later years, she being unaware of any happiness under grandpère's regime, tutelage; learning the hard way as she did, taught by Faust himself, it appeared.

Good as was (she was the first to admit it when mature) this bringing up by an old perfectionist, she knew, too, the nibbling frustrations and linked sausage-like continuous irritation that it produced in later life with people and things; the poltergeistic behavior, negative nuisances practiced by her contemporaries, her children, servants, Congress; the shiftless displacement, loss and breakage of objects; the casual vulgarness of nothing where it should be and nothing attended to; windows that would not open for a lack of simple planing, rusty spokes in bicycles, the disappearance of the screwdriver, the hot beds and cold frames neglected, angered her and tired her out in her attempt to set things right. So that when she was grown, and resembling him, sympathized, after the fact, as it were, she recognized that the things she had been critical of in him were due perhaps to cross circuits in her affection (grandmère's soft love) or respect (the aunts). He had not been unreasonable, but logical; in fact, as she still later concluded, that was just the trouble: grandpère was always right, which made him uncomfortable, everyone else corrupted to the circle, he alone remaining square. His annoyance when grandmère served a canned vegetable or soup if only once a year, Georgiana finally recognized as justifiable, the enormous garden provident enough, and the criticism she overheard of the old man's not letting cook have broilers or pullets was not stinginess or bad humor on his part, but a chicken fact, poultry common law, unthinkable to transgress: when the young roosters grown for eating were gone of course one did not massacre a potential layer and decidedly only an ignoramus would cut the throat of a laying hen. When grandpère's chicken-man once in a while culled his hens carelessly, if he suspected his error he cleaned the bird himself not trusting cook to hide the eggs which would be brought to light, evidence of crime. She wondered at 15 when she read "Tess" if this obvious animal crime had not influenced legal decisions, the rule of law being that a pregnant woman may not be executed; one more instance, then, of the doctrine of utility. Not quite so obvious but understandable, too, was grandpère's so-called extravagance, combined with what only looked like stinginess, i.e., the *best* of everything: expensive roosters, a pedigreed bull, a jewelled reel on his fly rod, etc.; at the same time, what she knew later as righteous indignation, at the least waste, whatever, and it was a pallid and shaky cook who witnessed from her kitchen window her own betrayal in the shape of a duckling head over heels for a bread crust spilled from a tilted carton on the back of the garbage man, grandpère standing by; with garbage itself a delicacy for the sow and bread crusts a delight for ducks (no left overs for layers however) grandpère's pain was excusable and his anger justifiable. As she learned, herself, eventually that the chief joy of farming was the unity of no waste; everything being usable as if in Heaven and this everlastingness a kind of transmigration, of the inert to the lively: garbage to pig, to bacon, etc., animal to manure to garden to aunts. An exception in perfection which brought no good results at all was grandpère's feeling for music: grandpère so terrified her with his horror, his actual doglike pain at discord, the slightest variation, that she dared not sing, quit whistling, the fear of a mistake so disconcerting her that the simplest melody was apt to go wrong with grandpère in a fury then and in genuine pain as if she had struck him. Music evades the fearful one and Georgiana met the evasion halfway, the only music left, in her speaking voice, which grandpère, himself, by constant criticism and quotations from Scripture taught her to modulate. Grandpère's occupational, avocational handiness became apparent in his speech, the figures of which developed from his own daily life. His "I'll break your spirit" to Georgiana when she defied him, pranced, as it were, kicked over the traces, took the bit in her teeth, etc., she understood, as well as his whittling language when he called her "cross-grained." She knew when she heard him say, "Oil and water won't mix," that it was a figure based on his own experience with a salad, although he could never teach the cook to keep the lettuce dry, much less understand the broader significance of the metaphor. Georgiana, too, learned to think and speak from touch. The more things she learned to do the easier it became to think and speak; riding, swimming, playing tennis, gardening, having children, raising dogs, sailing, all supplied her with similes, metaphors, analogies, even parables and she learned that every essential action was the same, really, with only a change of costume, and that gesture and thought, itself, was repeated *ad infinitum* in everything, everywhere, always; there are only a few stories; the difference descriptive, and things get clearer and clearer the further you get away from them, a kind of A No. 1 farsightedness or the actual disassociation of analogy.

One day in her wanderings, repeating her error of entering a room while in a daze, she entered grandpère's and gradually coming to but not quite, saw him in a position which never left her. It was comparable in its everlastingness with the image of Valentina's baby and like that one, if you remember, its significance never really became clear to her but the curiosity it engendered kept it alive; the queer question-mark confusion, all out of proportion, it seemed to her, with the circumstance, duplicated the scene of Valentina's sinful disturbance. Awakening slowly from her daydreams she found herself well into grandpère's room. Grandpère sat upright on the edge of the bed clad only in an undershirt; Georgiana clearly saw its texture, its warp and woof. Grandpère without a wing collar and scarf tie, it with one of three well known scarf pins, was odd in itself; grandpère's beard seemed higher up and out thrust; grandpère's head looked as if it were on a platter and his skimpy neck indeed resembled Valentina's baby's although that picture did not return at this misadventure; this one held its own by itself, and grandpère, upright and speechless, was enough and all. Grandpère's knees were knobby and naked and grandpère's legs amazed her because she had never realized he had any. And grandpère held something, it seemed, in his lap between his legs. What was it? He held it closely covered by the bottom end of his shirt. Could it be an early Christmas present she had surprised him in opening?

She tactfully thought of leaving. But why did he look at her with such hatred, such steady fury and self-control? This control, itself, was as unlike grandpère as his naked thighs and legs, his skimpy neck, and Georgiana stared steadily in bright wonder. It ended finally because it never would have otherwise in grandpère's calling out for grandmère to send the child away and bring him his clothes. Grandpère, it appeared, had mislaid his trousers, that was clear enough but why all the fuss, the white fury, and what was he holding outlined beneath his shirt? She kept her experience to herself feeling it was indeed secret but after this and even before there was something queer about grandpère, something unexplainable and unusual, symbolic, if she had known the word, about parts of grandpère. He never quite hung together after that; his smooth starched cuffs showing a little at the wrist reminded her of something else, but what? His pointed shoes, shiny and hard, delicate, pointing slightly outwards as he walked made her wonder what they really were. Weren't they something else? Not shoes? What did they mean? A queer curiosity arose about his cuffs, his pointed shoes. Grandpère had been just grandpère, a vague accepted feeling, now, as I say, parts of grandpère in themselves held Georgiana's attention, and these parts were secret, queer, meaningful. With beating heart she brought herself as she walked beside the old man one day, looking down at his fine sole leather shoes, to ask an indirect question, "Why, grandpère, do you toe, just a tiny bit, out?" Grandpère knew all the answers ordinarily but he, too, this time, seemed to sense a bigger question with a surer answer; neither of them, however, understood. He could only reply, "You, too, everyone toes out, you will, too, when you are grown up." This simple scene Georgiana recalled again and again when she was grown but having forgotten her strange symbolic curiosity she did not know why it stayed with her or why it had made such an impression. She was aware, however, as a child, of a gathering feeling of guilt which was unexplainable but clearly associated with grandpère, his shoes, his cuffs. His answer,

"You will, too, when you are grown up" which meant apparently nothing, came to her finally, however, as a significant answer, unintentional as it had been. And in her later life she began to see that things could mean other things, innocent and independent of what is intended and grandpère's answer came to mean without his being aware of any intention, "When you are grown up you will know all about sex." "Perhaps, but not quite," she was to add at this semi-clarification. At the end of the incident itself, the only apparent net result was that Georgiana took herself in hand and never of her own accord entered grandpère's room again, even crossing the hall to avoid it in passing; but no real censorship was conscious in her any more than in her avoidance of Mister Moon. She simply knew she must avoid both these things, unknown quantities though they were. But let us, too, avoid grandpère for a while.

The family doctor she did not avoid, but accepted from him the only innocent affection she had ever known or at least accepted. This man who had taught himself along with medicine a fine professional innocence really proved that innocence could be acquired. Georgiana's lack of censorship alone in her affection for him and her acceptance of his caresses was proof enough of his success. She loved the smell of him. She sat on his lap in front of everyone, enjoyed her special prestige with him, accepted his praise without embarrassment, even loved the burning feel of iodine because he introduced it. She really and truly ignored the sophisticated sneer of children a few weeks older than herself when she stood between the knees of Dr. Moore, his big, hard head pressed against her breast, his hands caressing her hips, and this thrilling absolutely innocent love came back to her with its attendant sweet smell of ether, faded roses and starch in her maturity and she deliberately ignored the facts of life in nostalgic desire but a brand new combination and insisted upon loving a strange man who reminded her of her past innocence.

*Chapter Four*

At about this time one of grandpère's houses, always kept in order but seldom rented, suddenly did, and grandpère dipped a few dollars worth into that precious principal for chinaware and slip covers, Puerto Rican rugs and kitchen utensils to content a tenant. It is a pleasure to write of Mr. Bullard. Any author could write most anything of him and it would be true: He was big, sand-colored, supple, free and easy, profane, a gentleman, hungry, a tease. He chose Georgiana from the first, picked her out, and in between anecdotes, jokes, stared at her as if he were amazed; as if he thought, "And where did you come from?" and, "What part will you play in my life?" It looked as if she barely came to his knee when they stood upright but at luncheon or tea he treated her as an equal and their eyes were level. Grandpère liked him, and so did the servants; he interfered with everything, advised the gardener, overtipped, stole the best peaches and strawberries, borrowed the few books grandpère had, placed the children's toys in lascivious positions for them to find upon awakening, did things the aunts had been taught were vulgar, but his gaze rested upon Georgiana. The family seemed to turn in unison and stare besides and she definitely gained prestige from the attentions of this monster. While the aunts' first shock at what they called vulgar was a stumbling block gingerly examined, soon vaulted, and with little shivers and miniature squawks they got over it. He treated them like girls and they watched him come and go from their windows dreaming retroactive dreams; Mr. Bullard was generous with his charm. "Women without love," Mr. Bullard said, "is pink lemonade without the pink." Mr. Bullard, gay, evil, recognized in Georgiana a companion; a little woman not only tolerant, forbearing, but admiring, loving; a little mistress, quite shy, but knowing, curious, generous, witty, fearless, gay, evil like himself. In this child who to the rest of her world appeared, and was, painfully shy, diffident, even cold, he saw something special that he did not wish to miss and he didn't. His first invitation to drive was more like a kidnaping. He wrapped her in rugs, didn't ask her permission or anyone else's, lovingly son-of-a-bitched, reprobated his thoroughbred and they were off. His mouth came down hard on hers; she had never been kissed on the mouth before and started to take away her lips as if it were over like a brief goodbye or greeting on the cheek. But Mr. Bullard without the use of his hands managed easily to keep her mouth on his and a determined movement forced her lips to cling to him as if for support; without knowing it she was doing the kissing; she could not let go without falling. Just as suddenly as he had begun he threw back his head leaving her suspended, and her mouth cooled in the rush of air as if she had added menthol or camphor ice to a chapped face. It was as if she were being gently chopped in two. The rest of the drive was as wild and exciting as she heretofore would have appreciated, the animal bolting, curving and teasing, snorting, waving his tail, shying at posts and paper bags, but for the next three weeks Georgiana was completely unaware of bolting horses, thunderstorms, family quarrels, punishment. Mr. Bullard's kisses stayed with her day and night and her background receded; her future limped away; her daydreams and dolls, her dogs, her troubles, sorrows, hunger, nightmares, fears, quite faded; disappeared; (she was comforted). Mr. Bullard came every day like an apple; it began to snow and he came in a cutter with bells. It was always the same: she turned up her face and he bent his head. He was not gentle, he hurt her, but for three weeks she lived in the present, the very kind of present that hard kisses give. She did not know what to do when she heard the announcement, "Mr. Bullard has gone." It seems that Mr. Bullard got fed up with a perfectly nice wife, two fairly intelligent children and a good cook so he got out his bicycle and rode into town forty miles away with nothing more than a sandwich and without making his will, and that was the end really and truly of Mr. Bullard. I don't know what he gained from his violent kissing courtship but Georgiana gained absolutely nothing except the three weeks she never lost. The shape of her face, her coloring, remained the same; the edges of her mouth returned to maiden-like smoothness as if the soft swelling caused by his kissing had never happened, and if she, too, was a deserted little wife she never acknowledged it and when Mrs. Bullard called for help she did not recognize any forlorn sistership. This funny love affair arranged itself like calcium from bone to tissue in the body and she came out even. It never reoccurred; no Mr. Bullard in modern dress appeared in her later life; in other words he just didn't make sense and ought probably to be left out of this story altogether. The shock of his departure preceded by a few hours the merciful *coup de grâce* practiced upon her favorite horse whose gentle nozzle breathed a little hole in the straw of his bed before he was carted away to be buried in a clearing of the woods where Georgiana visited twenty-four hours later to place some winter violets grown especially for her grandmother. The horse and Mr. Bullard went out of her life at the same time and she never thought of either again. At least not as such. But if she completely forgot Mr. Bullard she was forever critical of kisses and as for the horse winter violets made her cry when she was grown up.

As for the two surveyors, one dark and one light, each with piercing eyes, who spoke to her sister but looked at her, there is no doubt that the charm of their vitality staggered our heroine as if, grounded, lightning sped from head to toe and their week's sojourn, sleeping in the woods, losing themselves, whistling, singing, speaking a language she did not understand, giggling, wrestling, kidding, was a highlight, something out of a drawing too, in her terrain. Hired by grandpère to assure him of his boundaries, the expense of their stay on the debit side but a reassurance evidently of stability in the old man's mind, nevertheless, the two surveyors flirted with and made love to all the children, boys and girls, and then like rogues in an epic packed up and were off to new adventures. Georgiana never could place her guilt on the map of her soul as her childhood haunted her in later life because simultaneously with the passion for two surveyors, one light and one dark, came the petty larceny and bloody deeds of which she was actually guilty: the pleasure of stealing sugar lumps set out for tea on the sideboard; the added excitement of blood in her mouth from the hard granulated edges, may have been the real sin. At least it was sickening, sweet, terrifying, a pleasure that left her pale and shaking, and a plan each time formulating in her brain to repeat it, before it was even finished. Fifteen years subsequent, desperately ill in a Munich clinic, an outsized dose of opium mimicked in body and mind the sequence and sensations she had felt as a bad child, especially the thought, "I will do it again tomorrow," and her delight surprised an old nurse who thought she ought to be in pain, pitied her restlessness, patted her, gave her a sip of wine; dividends to her pleasure.

There was church of course every Sunday with its attendant variety of aches and pains, hunger, depression, melancholy, sweet smell of lilies, musty sunlight filled with particles of dust, stained glass angels, halos and a straddling Mary at the tomb, "He is not here, he has risen." Grandpère weeps and shivers at the thin sexless voice of the boy soprano and it is true the choir boy's voice, enhanced by the divine Episcopal acoustics of the airless and intimate dome of the little church seems to penetrate the ears of the congregation as if some sweet essence was being funneled into them, some thrilling serpentine knowledge. (Might they not all die of this angelic poison?) Grandpère could not bear the thin perfection of the boy's tone and his tears seemed not so much emotion as a reflex, a dog's pain at high notes. It was a good thing grandpère didn't know how to howl. During Mr. Bullard's regime Georgiana in the discomfort of too tight gloves and a hard hat that made her head ache would look at him for relief and he would roll his eyes at the ceiling, twirl his thumbs to amuse her and sometimes give a big bold wink. Georgiana felt a queer brotherhood but she was not amused. She waited for and remembered only his kisses and seemed hardly to recognize him in any other role.

And church over, the village idiot, charming lad with cerulean eyes, astral orbs, who began staring straight at Georgiana as he came toward her a long ways off, she returning his stare, each walking faster and faster until passing each other, she, with great control, contained herself, did not run, but he, poor lad, breaking into a fast trot and disappearing until the next time and repeat. Was the only difference between them her strict control, because she, too, wanted to run?

Not the least of her backdrop or her education were the animals. Some were a comfort to her; of others she was fearful; one she was forbidden: the bull. And in her little horoscope of symbols he became doubly to be avoided. Grandpère forbade

her to mention him as well as visit him and his red fearfulness
slowly took shape: he was sex. Grandpère forbade him and she
obeyed. Gradually she became grateful to the animal for staying
where he was, letting her know, as it were, where not to go,
leaving the whole world outside his pen to her. She climbed a
ladder and looked down on the huge undulating sows without
fear. She liked the opera of the barnyard fowls, the dry cackle of
the hens, the soft complaint of ducklings eyeing the ponds like
sailors fearful of sudden squalls, themselves of big nomadic turtles. Remember her heroic (to the barnyard) act when she heard
one scream, how she ran into the pond to her waist and lifted a
terrified duckling right out of the mouth of one of these horrors,
"Darling duck; I am coming; I will save you!" It flattened its
duck bill into her neck, tickling her; scrambled up into her hair,
weeping, explaining, still trying to get away, living it over and
over; poor little duck. Finally it went to sleep, but its foot was
chewed completely off, forever after a duck who couldn't understand, who disliked his mother, couldn't hold his friends; making
only semi-circular spirals in his travels, frowning and selfcon-
scious, often angry. Mr. Bullard called him Byron which was
cruel both to Byron and the duck. But Georgiana's pity and
affection for animals could not save her from cruelty to them,
that powerful variable. She watched steadily, her heart beating
hard, as the boy cousins fried a puppy, over, thank God, a cold
fire; he piteously whined as he lay on his side in the huge frying
pan, his pink stomach round with his greedily eaten supper, but
the children's eyes were bright. Their passion soon over, however, his joyous yippings and affectionate nibblings restored
them to their innocence and youth; only pretending, to finish
the game as usual, to carve him up with the sides of their hands
into drumsticks, second joints, etc., which made the puppy
almost mad with joy. Georgiana knew the sensuous pleasures
of this part of the game (to the puppy) herself, and she appreciated his, if translated, giggles. She did not join in the boys'
cruelties but to her shame practiced some of them alone. If there

had been a little priest in Georgiana's life her confessions would have included cruelty to a frog; she was not spared these primitive pleasures, nor the fever they induced, nor the calomel immediately administered to cure the fever; that queer mixed-up sequence that grownups ignorantly practice. Georgiana learned that punishment quickly follows pleasure and made a note of it. Without exactly saying it, she had a feeling of "you asked for it" when she sometimes accepted the pleasures, when she was grown up, of love, and never expected to get away scot-free, even when she was prepared for the sequence; in fact, she found it useless to prepare herself, when the variables were infinite, apparently, uncountable as dust. She also learned that punishment did not have to be "administered by," that it was like a verb without a subject, only an object, and that, herself; that it just happened and inevitably. Just as neither she nor the others made any attempt to escape grandpère when it was time to be switched (the lot of them could have torn him to bits!) neither did she ever question the authority of punishment.

Great-aunt Seraphina, dear elite, visited infrequently but with great effect, aplomb. Dressed in nth-power black (all the way through), mournfully, ghostly glamorous, she never stayed long enough to bore anyone, upsetting the regime as she did with the things she expected and graciously accepted, i.e., breakfast in bed, a room for her personal maid (a passionate Sinn Feiner), *café au lait* with matching silver pots, fruit by her bedside in the evening, a continuous tiny fire in her room. When beautiful, dignified, positively snooty Aunt Seraphina pulled up her voluminous skirts to warm her knees before the small meticulous fire Georgiana noticed with amazement every time the resemblance if not twinship of an old woman's pink dimpled knees to Valentina's, glimpsed while she scrubbed, and reflected in the shining surface of the floor she knelt on. This anatomical look-alike made her wonder and the reader will recall Walt Whitman's naughty observation. Georgiana looked and looked from Aunt Seraphina's knees to her face, making comparisons, thinking hard,

her features relaxing so that Aunt Seraphina wondered if she
could be stupid after all, this little Virginian whose grandmother
(her sister) had chosen to write her schoolgirl themes in Latin
and read Chitty's *Blackstone* for fun. The only reason that
grandpère put up with Great-aunt Seraphina's visits (remember
his hatred of Southerners) was that he had to. Aunt Seraphina
was as talented a tyrant as himself; they swapped tyrannies, as it
were, and out-stared each other; almost canceled one another,
as a matter of fact. Besides, these two actually admired each
other, naturally enough; admitted each other's good points, and
the two of them walked hand in hand, figuratively speaking,
through grandpère's rose garden, talking about insecticides and
comparing manures, superior in all things to the others who
accepted gracefully their own inferiority. Georgiana always remembered Aunt Seraphina's first-class contempt (and grandpère's mutual sympathetic aristocratic ditto) her pallor, as she
(Aunt S.) stood still one day on the bluestone path and related
to grandpère, quickly, to get it over with, the scandalous information, the *par exemple* of Patrick's daughter (Patrick, her
gardener) studying French. Georgiana remembered the little
flowers growing at their feet and the big dome of blue sky over
them; the two pale misunderstood aristocrats, *Patrick's daughter studying French*, and her own sympathy, at the time, for
Patrick's daughter, her equivalence and rights, while later, in-
heriting almost what she did not wish to inherit, her somewhat
diluted, at least divided, feelings on this matter, this sort of
matter; her sympathy for an Irish nursemaid of her own when
she said, "I can't eat out of those dishes (cheap blue willow-ware)
that people give the servants to eat off of, I throw up," her little-
girl insight but with it a grown-up inherited annoyance at this
fastidiousness in a little Irish maid when the dishes were very
pretty, and intact. Mr. Bullard, too, had admired the old man
(what a triumvirate the three would have made!) his spirit, his
bumptiousness so like his own; his lack of fear. He led him on as
a big boy does a little one made in his own image and destined to

be his like; he encouraged him in his figure-eights on the slipper-
iest ice, the kind that is black, thin and hard as a sheet of molasses
candy, and to race his stallion at an unhallowed clip, at those
times, as I have said, when the whole household in its nervous-
ness stopped doing what it was doing and did something else
until it was over (the old lady used to go to her room, lock the
door and thread needles); but Mr. Bullard would stand with his
binoculars at attention praising the action of the horse and the
behavior of the old gentleman. When it was over he would
usually whistle (whew!) and say, "A regular gentleman jockey!"
Georgiana, standing at his side, blushed every time he said it and
always believed that, praise as it undoubtedly was, it was praise,
nevertheless, between man and man, something she shouldn't
hear, of some sort of physical prowess outside of which women
and girls could only wander; she felt that the word jockey was
a sexual compliment. All her life she made these unexplainable
literary errors and all her life she blushed at words. Georgiana
was the only one of the children that Aunt Seraphina could put
up with and she was often sent for to be talked to; to be sent
away just as abruptly when the old lady found her tiresome or
unresponsive. Georgiana never quite solved the problem of Aunt
Seraphina and Oscar Wilde. Aunt Seraphina as a child had sat
on Oscar's lap but he was not to be mentioned by her, Georgiana,
at all, ever, because of his proclivities. Georgiana wondered what
else Aunt Seraphina had done on Oscar Wilde's knee and confused, besides, his proclivities with something meaning his nose
which made it even harder. In her imagination the great-aunt
sitting on the bad man's lap was not very prepossessing especially
as although she could reduce her aunt in size she could not
picture her any more youthful in appearance so that the whole
composition looked, I suppose, more or less as the current
photographs of Mr. Morgan in the courtroom look to us. But
what had Aunt Seraphina done on his knee? She gazed at the
highborn profile and wondered and wondered. No answer came.
Neither did she ever find out why she shouldn't read George

Moore's *Brook Kerith* and to this day thinks it must be the story of a bad girl for whom she has always felt the deepest sympathy. To this day the books forbidden by both Aunt Seraphina and grandpère (Sudermann's *Dame Care*) remain unread (fortunately it was a small and arbitrary list) and Georgiana blushes at Oscar's name, ashamed apparently, of the unknown. Just as she left unread these books, certain words all her life had no meaning to her, eluded her, as I have said. It was as if she had been forbidden words, too, innocent as they were: lyric, reciprocity, notary public, auspices (a tent?); and in spite of a brilliant vocabulary when she was older her friends were curious when she genuinely asked the meaning of a simple word and at once forgot so that confronted again, unable again to understand, she would say "what is a lyric?" "I don't know what harbinger means." This funny kind of everlasting obedience had its little rewards and she was always curious, always sure of something special underneath things like in an Easter egg hunt and she was never surfeited, bored, became a sort of intellectual with a pathetic belief in the abstract. During all the half-hours Georgiana sat with Aunt Seraphina she never dared ask her about her father and Aunt Seraphina as if she were on her honor not to, finger on lips, never mentioned him, favorite nephew though the rest of us knew him to be. This everlasting secrecy, this conspiracy, it seemed to her, against the beautiful father of her imagination bore inedible fruit in the sense that Georgiana fed herself on daydreams, sustained herself in make-believe, lived in an affectionate nowhere with a handsome stranger, and a queer sort of Oedipus-search developed as she hunted with bandaged eyes, as it were, for a lover in later life who resembled the one she had never seen, which was to confuse her as we have suggested, and create a mistake which wasted a lot of her love-making time. A faded photograph became in her mind an exact likeness in great detail, enhanced and honored in her imagination, restored, so that there is no doubt at all that she recognized him in others when she grew up and felt an immediate desire for each as any other girl does for the callow youth or exceptional adult who reminds her of the first man in her life. Georgiana's first love was invisible; but irresistible, an able and darling ghost. And if only the other men in her life had hid themselves, how much simpler and all-of-a-piece, how logical and sweet would have been her career. This ambitious nostalgic love for some one who did not exist gave her the upper hand, taught her a kind of active rather than passive love, a dislike of interruption, and without her knowing it the wish to love rather than be loved, so that voluntarily, nevertheless, in spite of later complaints, she became in the end an unrequited lover because that is what she wanted. Grandmère, too, that silent old lady who timidly, sporadically, and unsuccessfully defended her, instilled in her an uneasy fear of being loved, the fear of causing pain, an irritable fear of the loss of her little freedom. Grandmère's sorrowful looks when she was unsatisfactory, her undeserved, she felt, rewards when she was amenable, tore at her conscience, pecked at her heart, even her muscles, bones, blood vessels, gave her tonsillitis, and she found that defending herself against this sort of painful affection was harder than resisting the others who did not love her; the latter strengthening her, the former weakening her. Grandpère had priority in punishment but grandpère's punishments, Dantesque, peculiar to him, she accepted without question; her grandmother's, seldom, less intentional, were strange, weakening, not in keeping either with grandmère or any cosmos she earlier or later knew. And Georgiana felt that they were a punishment against grandpère, too, which mingled her disgust with remorse. Suddenly, each time, faced with his little granddaughter in her nightdress, frightened and pale but steadfast, coldly angry, a little future image of himself without the beard, how must the old man have felt! Punished, I am sure. Perhaps they each would have liked to give up the steadfastness and hug each other, "Why must this happen to us!" Why did grandmère choose as a punishment against Georgiana to bed with grandpère? Why shouldn't it have been a reward? The old man lay still and Georgiana lay bravely beside him for the allotted time. Each might have wept but neither did and only a finicky horror came of this indecisive union with grandpère for Georgiana. Crawling out and tiptoeing away without goodnight she lay the rest of the night after these sporadic experiences without any feeling whatever, a kind of aftermath that could be deducted without loss from her little biography, unable to remember what it was, even, that she was not to do again. If pins had been stuck into her from top to toe I think she would not have felt a thing; so sensitized was her whole body that it became numb.

Like a little "Nora" but for no specific reason Georgiana in time of stress ran out of the house, slamming the door, raced into nowhere, darkness, in a kind of dress-rehearsal panic, symbolizing not so much the plus-sign desire for freedom as the minus-sign wish to evade the emotional tentacles of sentiment, love, hate, incest, and returned inexplicably each time to just that. We find this very act, this little trip reenacted again and again in her grown-up love life and if she does not in effect actually leave the premises, run away to return in humiliation, she nevertheless does that very thing. And just as in her childhood this useless peripatetic, ending in repeated capitulation (the old folks, in a kind of hand-me-down wisdom predating Freud, refusing to follow) gained her nothing and she thought she never could win and it is true she always lost. But lost, she was the searching party, too, which kept her on her toes, as it were, and grandpère never really broke her spirit though he taught her with his sinister patience her gaits. Grandpère being, it appears, the croupier and Georgiana like an everlasting patron of the place, who never would learn what the croupier knows: the presence of one zero makes it impossible to win.

# Part Two

ＳEVERAL YEARS
have passed. Our heroine is thirteen and I give you part of her
journal. I am amazed at its objectivity until I remember that
she had from the beginning a literary ability (a way of talking
to herself) as well as the power of observation. That is all you
will find here but it is not important that the reader pry into the
life of an adolescent, because, as I have said elsewhere, it is of no
consequence. Unless you find the journal amusing you may
skip it.

Grandpère dipped too often into his principal; taxes tripled;
cousins had to be sent to preparatory schools; the stables were
sold; the hounds died of old age and were not replaced (with

the exception of Bonny, a kind of everyday dog, without a pedigree, mentioned herein). Grandpère never bought on margin but worthless stock bought and paid for was still worthless; the big place with its handsome acres was sold but never paid for; grandpère moved his queer dependents into the New House (the very one he had let to Mr. Bullard), held on to a few of the deepest lots, put in a new batch of precious fruit trees, added some cold-frames, took along a faithful gardener, bought a very expensive motor because he had to have the best, and just managed to send the girls off to school without ever telling anyone until after he was dead, when it became apparent, that he was practically broke; refusing to admit, even to himself, that he was living on credit, exactly as those southern gentry he most despised had done for so long and so genteelly.

Some boys, beaux for the girls, have trickled in as grandpère gets older and tireder; there is a little fun but not too much; the young old aunt has taken over, more and more resembling grandpère who had once made her behave herself, herself.

And so we present this bean-like girl in a long quote, as it were, to avoid the miscegenation, confusion of pronouns, and so forth, inherent in biographical data, no matter how cautious, and, as I have said, the reader may skip it. Our heroine finally does.

Chapter One

THIS IS MY
first day at school, away from home, boarding school. I have not
been very frightened. My sister, of course, has been here before
me, and my mother graduated from this school, and her sister. I
know, therefore, a lot about it. My sister is the prettiest girl that
anyone has ever seen, and everyone has always said that my
mother was beautiful and good. Everyone loved her, but I have
no remembrance of her. After all, I was six months old when she
died, and then my father, six months later. I am supposed to look
very like my mother, except she had blue eyes, mine are black,
and no one has ever called me beautiful or even pretty; certainly
I am not good. I have a wicked temper, and I hate people, quite

a few almost constantly. My grandfather has often told me that I am cross-grained and horrid like my father. I have cried about that, but I have cried proudly. I know quite well that my father was a superior person. I have heard my great-aunts, his aunts, say so. He was proud and gay and sometimes quite wicked. He was a Virginian. My grandfather, who is a New Englander and a gentleman, I think has never forgiven my father who was a Virginian and a gentleman for marrying my mother. Some of this I have gathered, but some of it I know to be true. My father did brave and sudden and sometimes shocking things. He answered people back. He acknowledged neither age nor position. He was very good-looking, according to my great-aunts (and a beautiful picture I have of him). He was six feet two inches tall with very dark eyes and hair. He was too thin. His very beautiful little sister whom he adored and whom my mother resembled died quickly of tuberculosis. My father's father died too of tuberculosis but slowly. They said it was a bullet in his lung from the Civil War. He was the handsomest man in Virginia. Everyone admitted that. "We are a good-looking lot," my great-aunt has said to me quite often. Yes, Aunt Seraphina thinks even I am pretty, but I sometimes think it is a pride in beauty and breeding that she has and she will not see a lack of either in me. We have descended from distinguished people, but I am half Yankee. My great-aunt grows stern and pale and so does my other great-aunt when they refer very seldom and always indirectly to this sinister fact. It is not exactly distinguished to be half Yankee as I am; and Aunt Seraphina has looked at me searchingly and said, "You are like your father, although I believe your mother's family were gentlefolk. Your grandmother was very quiet, but certainly your grandfather was a gentleman and I liked having him here. He loved my roses." When Aunt Seraphina speaks like this I grow hot with resentment and what is probably loyalty to my grandfather. She has a lot of white hair brushed up from her round forehead which is high and clearly white too. Her nose turns up and away from everything, especially Yankees, and I cannot describe her face except that it, too, is white. I do not know the color of her eyes, and her expression is sometimes so strained and sometimes so young and charming that it is difficult to describe her at all. I have spent days alone with her, always it seems opposite her in the dining room with only the width of an ancient refectory table between us. On the walls are flat valuable Japanese prints which I cannot see because four gold cherubs light up only our faces from beneath and there is a square of white cloth. Dinner has lasted until long after my New England bed time. Annie, ancient too and Irish, in the family for forty years, with eyebrows incredibly high, unconscious mimic of her mistress, brings us pink shrimp with bits of transparent armor still clinging to them before they are dipped in pink sauce, and a clear soup barely covering a pleasant little pattern underneath. "Annie — a tablespoon of wine in Miss Georgiana's glass." I do not care for the taste of it, but it makes me feel pink in the face. Aunt Seraphina is very distinguished, no doubt of it, but she ought to hear the way my grandfather can say, "Southerner" with scorn. Whatever is bad in me is easily explained: Southern blood, unstable, undisciplined, hot-tempered. How hot-tempered my grandfather can get over my hot temper. I believe he loves me, but I don't know why I think so. I know he loved my mother very much. I cannot take her place. I am neither beautiful nor good.

*Chapter Two*

THIS HAS BEEN
my second day at school. Yesterday bothers me a little. Last night
I was excited and could not go to sleep. I was sleeping nicely when
the first bell rang this morning. I jumped up and looked around
for yesterday's clothes. I was dressed a long time before the
warning bell rang. My room-mate woke up then, dashed some
cold water on her eyelids, put on a wool dress over her head as
her nightie slipped down over her feet. Stockings and slippers
took only a second; murmuring, "Damn, it's morning," she was
down the two flights to breakfast and naked under her dress she
was bowing her head to "Bless-Oh-Lord-this-food-to-our-use-
and-to-thy-service-for-Christ's-sake-Amen." I trembled out-

side, late to breakfast the first morning. But yesterday. A group of old girls surrounded me. "It's Caroline's sister." I felt self-conscious in my new traveling dress. It is blue serge. It fits me from throat to knees and I have neither breasts nor hips. I simply go in a lot at the waist and my legs are very long below my skirt. There is an infinitesimal curve to them and my ankles are not lumpy only perceptible. I have on my first high heels which push up the arches of my feet and make me feel taller than I am and even thinner. I am very thin, but I am glad that my bones are no bigger than those of a chicken and only serve to hold me together. I have on shiny silk stockings, also my first. There are six pairs of them slippery and delicious in my trunk. My hair is in two braids not very thick, quite black, and very fine. Some phenomenon makes single strands of it stand out from the rest. I am ashamed of its hanging down. The girls who are staring at me are all grown up. Their hair is done in hair-dos. My sister is there too. She seems proud of me but I am not sure. Jean is there: her room-mate. She has pink hair, pink cheeks, a little heart-shaped face. She is as tall as I am and as thin. She has on a grass-green smock, embroidered, tight at the wrists. She is six-teen. She has assurance. "Why, Caroline, she is prettier than you are but she is black. She is a little nigger." The girls disap-pear. My room-mate looks at me. "How much allowance do you get?" My little patent leather bag lies open on my bureau. I dis-cover in it the stub of my railroad ticket, my handkerchief still folded, but the clean new five-dollar bill, my allowance for a month, is gone. My room-mate is watching me. My heart sinks and I want to cry. What shall I write home? I hear my room-mate saying, "Of course it was Frieda; she was in here with the rest. Everyone knows she's like that. She rooms down the hall. You'll never get it back."

Classes began at two o'clock. Bells rang every ten minutes because of course they were only introductory classes to show us which room English and French and Geology were in, that is all, and give us our books. There is a small shop at the head of the stairs for pencils and things. Miss Pinkerton keeps it. We stood in line. It was fun buying pencils, an eraser, copy books, and a loose-leaf notebook, a French dictionary, and some pads. All these things we could charge, and I shall not miss my five dollars until I want a soda. I watch Miss Pinkerton as I stand in line. We extend out into the hall and down the stairs. There is a lot of chatter between the old girls and giggling. They kissed each other a lot when they came and now they stand about with their long arms dangling around each other's necks. Miss Pinkerton is very serious and hands out things to each girl without looking at her. She has fine black hair along her upper lip. I suppose she is twenty-five, and she has little separate pointed teeth because her upper lip is drawn back tight and shows them. She looks exactly like a cat. Someone behind me says, "I wonder if Mary Susan is back yet." Another girl answers in a low tone, "Of course she is. She and Pinkerton came together. What do you think?" I met this Mary Susan later. I was on the way upstairs. She was just ahead of me. She had an armful of books — brown-haired, boy's face, poised, mature. She must be eighteen. She heard me behind her, turned and looked at me as she reached the top. "Hello," I said. She stared at me and said in a drawl, "Oh, hello," and then, "Fresh." Tears came into my eyes at this unfair pronouncement. "I'm Mary Susan," she said. "I suppose you're Caroline's kid sister," and she went on to her room down the hall. My room-mate says, "You are not supposed to speak first to Seniors." I'll never speak to her again at all. I guess I hate her.

*Chapter Three*

*T*HIS ISN'T A
fashionable school. My grandfather would not send us to a fashionable school. We are ladies already he says and we don't have to
go to a school that makes them. There is a fashionable school not
far from this one. The girls go on Sunday to St. John's Church
where we go, too; in a long line with two or three teachers and
Miss James who is our head mistress. The girls at that school are
all rich and come from the Middle West which is supposed to
be a pretty awful combination, but I think the girls are prettier
in that school than ours. This is an Episcopalian school, and there
are lots of ministers' daughters here. They are quite awful and
they stick together and would not think of getting up and playing about at night. Playing about at night is fun. There is a
teacher opposite our room, but once we get by her door it is

simple to fly on bare feet to any room we choose. I love it. It is exciting. At nine-thirty lights go out and we are supposed to go to sleep but that is when our eyes begin to shine like cats'. Once you get into someone else's room the idea is to snap under a bed because often all at once the door opens and Fräulein's voice in the dark says, "Someone is here. Who is it? Answer me." I can't even shiver; there isn't room. Packed close to me are two other girls terrified, wishing they hadn't come, but I love it. I pinch one of them hoping to hear her squeal. They smell sweetly of powder. Fräulein feels for the light, and the two girls in their beds blink and rub their eyes, pretending, as she screws up the bulb, and the room is brilliant. "What — oh my, we were asleep. Fräulein, I am asleep."

"Nonsense, come out!"

"Cowards" I whisper to my close companions as both of them crawl out, leaving their powdery smell.

"Five demerits. Go to your rooms at once."

I lie flat against the wall, cold, happy. I will not come out, and teachers do not bend down to look under. It is undignified if no one is found.

"What have you got to eat?"

"Nothing, go away. Shhh, you'll be caught."

But I am not afraid. I am famished.

"What have you got?" I insist in a whisper.

"Cheese."

"Goody."

"Here. No knife. Here is my shoehorn."

"Have you got an orange? Give it to me and I will go away."

Those two, what are they afraid of? Shut the window; I am cold. There is a creaking sound. Who is that on the fire escape? A giggle, and it's Dotty crouched in her nightie absolutely naked apparently because of the light from behind. A great globe of a street light shines right through her. You can almost see her bones. One or two passing below are merely black. I am delighted because here is someone who is fun and who isn't afraid. "Are you hungry? Come in quickly." "No. A feast in Rosa's room. I saw in the window. The pigs, not to ask me. Nor you, Georgiana." "But we don't ask them to ours. Shhh, let's go to it anyway. Wait." I climb shaking with the cold and excitement out to the flimsy fire escape, holding Dotty's hand. We sneak along, past a window open wide, and dark inside. I stick in my head and call, "Boo." A squeal from inside and my heart stops. It's that silly Janie. Little idiot. Hysterical little fool. She'll have Miss James after us. We clutch each other and wait for lights and voices. Nothing happens. Far off downtown we can hear a late trolley.

"Look at the stars," I whisper. "Dotty, look at those terrible awful wonderful stars." One of them streaks through the sky as I look.

"Get in here." Dotty hauls me over a window sill. There is no light except from the outside and inside we find dimly about six girls. They aren't pleased to have us. It is a conservative group — feasts, yes, but they have asked permission. They are trying to have fun and obey the rules at the same time. It can't be done. How disgusting to be such cowards. "We promised not to make any noise." "Please." "Oh please." "Shhhhh." There is great hulking Rosa squatting in the dark with something special she's brought there. Saps. I'm sure it's something good. I'm starving but I say, "Come on Dotty. Good-bye pigs. Go to the devil. Eat your lousy caviar. Beeep." "Oh, shhhh." "Oh nuts." Dotty and I climb out again. "Pigs." "Idiots." "Nasty little sluts."

I am finally in my own bed again. It is badly made and as I pull up the blankets my feet stick out. I assume angles. I finally begin to warm myself up. Less and less of the sheet is cold. I am laughing to myself. What fun. My room-mate's bed is empty. Still out. I am asleep. I awake later with a sharp pain in my side. "Oooooh." My room-mate is looking down at me. "What is the matter?" "Oooooh I can't breathe." "Where?" My room-mate puts her hand under my nightgown. "Where?" "Here." I place her hand just under my right breast. "Please," I say. "Yes," she says, 'is it better?" "It's gone." "Idiot, fool, to run around with nothing on." I am asleep again.

OH WELL, AT least I am not a new girl any longer. I have already been home for Thanksgiving vacation. I did not want to go home and I am glad to be back again. A teacher went with us. It is very involved crossing New York. From the Grand Central Station to the Pennsylvania is really impossible. I don't know how it is done. I did not look.

Page is our chauffeur. He met us. He has a big mouth and high pink cheekbones. His eyelashes stick out and his eyes are pale blue. His sister is a schoolteacher in the village. He wants to be a fireman in New York. He wears a ribbed black uniform and his puttees show that he is a little bowlegged. But I don't mind this when I am sitting beside him. I talk to him and laugh brightly. He blushes and goes faster. There is practically nothing on the straight flat road to our house. I smell leaves burning and we turn in behind thick evergreens and barberry. My dog licks my face. I turn my cheek clear around to my ear and my Aunt does the same. My grandfather's short white beard tickles me. It is unpleasant. My grandmother I hug, however, with some pleasure. It embarrasses and pleases her. She turns away. "Very well, behave yourself then." Little white curls on her forehead never seem to move. Always there, always forever. Black lace over her bosom, a very old cameo, Italian. There is a story about that. Vaguely I gather it though my grandmother has never mentioned it to me. Tonight before dinner I shall be called in to fasten a fragile necklace as my grandmother stands straight before her mirror. And I shall see next to her bureau her sewing basket and in it a little packet of letters from me. Only a few. Such a few. I am sorry. "Dearest Grandmère," they begin. Molasses candy with hard white nuts for me and gingerbread with raisins. I know which cupboard.

I am supposed to greet the cook.

"How do you do, Mary."

"It's taller than ever you are. You'll never be as good-looking as your mother. Her face was like a seashell."

A turkey, lying on its back, its stubby legs apart is half sewn up between them. Its neck is turned aside as if it were resting on a pillow. I stare at it and then I go out in the garden. The grape arbor is bare; the cold frames empty. The flowers are gone but the paths are neatly kept and straight. Along the side of the garden is a row of chicken houses. There are hundreds of white Wyandottes strutting, scraping, clucking. High wiring separates each silly proud rooster from another and his flock. Silly proud rooster. I suppose he thinks he is to be envied his harem of plump pullets. For no apparent reason he suddenly picks up his spurred feet and lopes to a neighboring yard. With tall red comb sway-ing he throws himself against the wire at his fancied rival next door. Soon his white neck is bloody and he quits. The hens scatter and he struts to the drinking fountain — drinks deeply — eyes his ladies with a beady eye — comb rakish — makes a pass at one of them. Screams and they all run around in circles as though it weren't inevitable. Choosing one at random, he sits on her. Feathers fly. Raucous clucking. He pecks viciously at her head with his long beak. "Hateful thing, Shoooo," I cry, beating on the wire, but he has finished and stands up. He begins scratching for food. The chicken world is comparatively quiet. Henry comes along the path, the gardener, pushing a little wheelbarrow with two shovels of red dirt in it. He puts it down and takes off his hat. He never used to take off his hat, but I am taller now. I suddenly remember something. I dash back to the house and around the corner of it. Yes, of course, two barrels of apples, greenings and pippins. Greenings are always damp and give way easily to the teeth, but a pippin is good, delicious, resists every bite to the end, and I batter it to pieces with pleasure. It is cold and sweetly sour. I hurl the core as far away as I can into the field.

I am followed into the house by my dog, Bonny, who snuggles up to me as I lie on the couch and breathes damply in my neck. Darling sweet Bonny, I love him. She is a bitch, but for seven years since we have had him, we have called him "him" and "he"; it's Grandpère's idea. Poor Bonny with long and indecisive tail and soft brown velvet ears. He has often slept in my bed with me, warm at my feet on cold nights, licking my toes. God knows how he manages to breathe. There are guests for tea. The Simpsons, all of them. Dr. and Mrs., Allyn and Crispin. Allyn and Crispin have on T shirts and sneakers. It's smart to be a little bit dirty, anyway Allyn and Crispin are. And once I saw them clean in top hats avoiding the top of a taxi door as well. In town, of course. Allyn is older. He is an engineer. He doesn't take his eyes off Caroline my sister for a moment. She is sitting in a three-cornered chair, her ankles crossed, high heels, soft blond hair braided, folded up against her neck, very pretty. Her cheeks are pink and white. She has stolen some water-color paint of mine, black, and dipping a match in water has blacked her long eyelashes. They are a little stiff. Devastating. Caroline's eyes are always light blue in the morning but toward late afternoon the pupils begin to grow large and by night in artificial light they fill up the entire eye and her eyes become as black as mine. Mine are really very dark brown with a black edging. Caroline's nose is small and turns down a tiny bit at the end. She hates it but it is distinguished and without it she might look like those awful magazine covers. I must admit that in the winter when we go skating there is a little white spot where the nose dips downward, and with bright pink cheeks on either side it looks rather unexplained. I am always the same color all over, hot or cold. It is very boring. I have heard it called olive but I really am brown with a light underneath. I am that way all over. I have stood on a chair to see the lower half of me in the mirror. It is nice to see oneself half at a time that way. It is not so embarrassing. As for the top part, if I fold my arms over my head, I can plainly count my ribs. If I stretch and hold my breath only my spine seems to hold me together like that of an insect. There is a little fine etching of hair under each arm, very shiny, and each of my small breasts is stamped the size of a quarter with mauve. The lower half of me is very long, very slender, and straight. There is a curve, however, from a small triangle beneath my stomach to below each knee, where curves dip in to swell out again just a little, allowing me a calf from the front. No matter how I try to close my legs, it is impossible. Each leg is decidedly separate from the other. There is a half-inch, then two inches, then an inch again of wallpaper all the way down barely disappearing at the knees and just at the ankles. From the side my buttocks are round and high and my thigh that dips in where it joins my body jumps out again and falls back gradually to the knee. My body is lovely. It shines like satin. I don't know about my sister's. I have never seen it. We have adjoining rooms and the same bath but we always lock the door. Last year Caroline got in somehow and stared at me in the tub. I cried. She laughed at me.

I practically forgot the tea party but it wasn't any fun with Allyn staring at Caroline that way and me staring at him. His face is very brown from a summer on the Bay and his hair is cropped short and waved tightly. It is gold color and the ends look on fire in the light. There is a little gold hair on his face, too, and his mouth is drawn back showing straight teeth, a little blue and transparent. He looks as though he might bite. He is delighted with Caroline and she knows it. She keeps saying, "It's disgusting, really disgusting. School is lousy." All *I* want is to get back there, prowling around at night, sick with giggling, aching with suppressed laughter. I turn suddenly and find that dark-eyed Crispin is as intently watching me as I am Allyn and Allyn my sister. My hair is still down, rather stringy at that and nobody has ever looked at me, if Caroline was there first. I suppose I am jealous. I know perfectly well I am jealous. My throat hurts with it and my eyes sting. The ends of my fingers hurt unbearably. She is lovely. Dr. Simpson puts his arm around me. "This one is getting too tall for you, Crispin." I stand straight in his arm. "Can you still whistle?" At this I feel the blood rush to my cheeks though it does not appear. I hate to whistle. My grandfather loves to hear me whistle to the victrola, unless of course I make a mistake! I have done it by the hour, my grandfather listening in the hall. Any tune new or old, any opera, any aria. I have no memory for music but I can anticipate the most difficult arrangement and I am always on the key though I have no idea what a key is. I will not do it for company. My mouth pursed up I look too silly. What a kid I am to Allyn and Crispin. I am ready to cry. "Come," says my grandfather. "Please," I say, "oh please, I can't whistle a bit well, really Grandpa, please." "Let her off," says my grandmother, timidly. The Simpsons are gone away in their noisy old Pierce. My grandfather looks me in the eye, "Cross-grained!"

# Chapter Five

*Y*ES, REALLY I am glad to be back. I wonder what is homesickness. It seems to be a very definite illness. There is a little new girl called Vera who is really ill. Her eyes are always red with weeping and the house mother goes in and out of her room with half glasses of spirits of ammonia. Vera is so small that she looks out of drawing in an ordinary landscape. She is a minister's daughter and she keeps enormous diaries. Her mother has been notified she is so home-sick. Anything starts her, especially at prayers. A mournful hymn and she goes out like a candle. Prayers is pretty awful. At night after dinner we make a dash and a slide over polished floors for hymnbooks. We all stand around in the library two or three deep. It's not so good being in the front row in case you get a pinch from behind. Miss James looks twice as big as any of us. Her mouth is closed tightly and her big plain black eyes are twice as big as they really are through glasses that magnify for her as well as to us. We are all scared by those inky eyes. She has an unhealthy pale fat face. An old girl told me that she drinks forty cups of coffee a day. She looks around at us now in prayers and we all drop our eyes before that glance, even the teachers. Fräulein, deceitful-looking with dyed black hair, shifts her weight from one foot to another and licks her lips. Mam'selle isn't really afraid. She only smiles sarcastically and sways her hips a little. Mam'selle is wonderful. She has favorites among the girls and they are always the prettiest and girls with style that she chooses. They must be chic. She never scolds them in class as she does the others, really loses her temper, I mean. I think she likes me even if I am not sophisticated like her other favorites. She has a wide mouth with big teeth. She has a brown coarse skin and a wide high-cheeked face like pictures of peasants. She has desperate blue eyes. Her hair is bright yellow and she wears to class mostly a magnificent open-work lace blue dress with a low neck in front. We can see the beginnings of her breasts which are wide apart. I feel that she is laughing at me. She gives the impression of having seen the world and is amused. I am attracted to her. She has long knotty fingers with rings that are too loose. Sometimes in the late afternoon, just before study hour when one or two of us have come in early and reported to her, as teacher on duty, what is in each little bag that we may carry: six oranges, a half pound of hard black gumdrops; she will sit at the piano or stand up over it and with two fingers play dashing staccato little French tunes, tapping with a large foot in a big blue slipper and swaying her head. Sometimes she will sing the words. They are naughty and I don't know what they mean. She laughs at my intent rather than jolly interest and stops playing to pinch my cheek. It hurts.

"*Au tableau*, Georgiana," and I write down irregular verbs

and *bal, carnival*, and all that. I am excited under Mam'selle's electric glance. I never make a mistake. She is glad. She shows me off. Not that some of the others don't know their endings, too, but they have sweated blood for it and stayed up nights; they are grinds and keep notebooks. Mam'selle detests them and brings them to the board one at a time, asks them impossible questions, speaks sarcastically and bitterly to them, has them in tears. Then she does fly into a temper. She is disgusted. Class is dismissed. We file out, all of us frightened, even the favorites. We don't risk a word or ask about tomorrow's lesson.

Prayers is over and my knees hurt. René at the piano has started a dance tune. This is the most fun of all. Only about twenty minutes to go before evening study hour. I do love it. Whom shall I ask to dance or who will ask me? Only a few of us are good dancers. Yes; here comes Fredericka sliding toward me bumping people. She is long-legged, thin, a little bony. She is a country girl right off the farm, Connecticut Yankee. She has sleek brown hair and flat bangs. She would rather dance with me than anyone. She asks me days before to save her a dance. "Georgiana, here we go. I insist on leading." The teachers around the wall stare at us. We dance well, very close together. Fredericka, a little taller than I, holds me so tight that I cannot speak. Her strong long arm encircles my waist a time and a half. I am bent back like a bow. Our thighs are close at every move; our knees interfere pleasantly. Our feet nimbly avoid each other. How nice. Fredericka's face is pink, mine still pale. We clap and clap. "More, René." "More please." "There's only a second." No one dares cut in on Fredericka and me. Several girls are furious and won't look at me. I promised them a dance but it is too much fun dancing with Fredericka. The room is hot. We do not speak.

"Brrrr," the bell for study hour. Fredericka gives me a hug, keeps her arm around me as the music stops. "No wonder the boys love you. You are so thin at the waist." Her eyes are shining and she is pretty. She is sixteen. I don't know what she means. There are no boys.

Study hour at night is a bore or at any time for that matter. There isn't anything to do. I wish I were a senior and could study in my room. Then I could fry eggs in cold cream — not bad by the way — and eat asparagus tips out of a tin. There is nothing to do down here but watch the clock. I have a couple of study periods during the day and that is more than enough to learn my lessons. Botany and stuff like that I do in the five minutes before class. English is too easy. Latin is hard to bluff but an hour a week and a word written out here and there over the original and I am way ahead as it is. What to do. I look around; brown heads, fair heads, pigtails, bare napes, wisps sticking out. Faces still flushed from dancing, here and there eyes looking up and meeting mine, a grin or two. Chessie Brooks over there with a big geology book up in front of her and inside a *True Story*. I don't like her. She really is disgusting. Her hands are always hot; she has shiny red lips and prominent rolling eyes. My room-mate says she is terrible, really awful, always talking about boys. Two want to marry her, she says. She comes from Cleveland. Her father makes silk. She's rich. My room-mate says that she can't decide which of the two boys to marry. My room-mate says that she says that both boys love her terribly. But she says that the second one is terribly passionate. The first one would wait a little while but the second one would be on top of her the first night. What in the world?

*Chapter Six*

THIS HAS BEEN Sunday. It is about the most difficult thing at school to get out of going to church and I didn't today although I actually felt queer about half-past ten. I have a very sweet little blue velvet hat that is diamond shaped and sits on my forehead. It has a very small silver bird on the side. I only wear it on Sunday and I wear my hair up like the others except the very little ones, of course. The teachers go along with us like guards. We march along on our high heels. We are not allowed to go arm in arm to chuch. It is quite a walk and across the green to St. John's, and passing motorists take a good look at us. Some of the men stare into our faces and open their big mouths and say something to each other.

Sometimes we hear the laugh that follows. I wonder if I have a hole in my stocking. Approaching the church in another long line at right angles are the Westchester School girls. They have come in busses; there must be a hundred of them. We sometimes meet and mingle every other one at the entrance but we never speak, even though some of us know one or two of them. Lots of them have on fox furs and smart suits. Only one of us has a fox fur and that is Jenkins from Des Moines. Even Chessie Brooks hasn't one. She says her sister has one though and she is going to have one for Christmas or bust. I hope she will bust. Church is very hot and still. We crowd into our pews at the side of the side aisle. The Westchester girls have two whole front pews. We kneel at once and my room-mate's curly hair tickles my forehead. She pinches the back of my leg. "I have some gum."

"Look out for Fräulein." We are up in our seats again and I look around furtively. The first eyes I meet are Fräulein's. She looks furious. We are up singing a hymn. My room-mate sounds ridiculous. It is great sport to sing the words of the second verse instead of the first. I start singing the third, quite loud in a clear voice. My face is very hot with pleasure at this sport. One or two of the other girls recognize our game and join us. Two or three people turn around. Janie has a terrible fit of the giggles and her face is bright red. She has to sit down and Fräulein is white with rage. The hymn is over and now for quite a while we get up and sit down again. I make all the responses and move automatically. I am thinking of all sorts of things. My head aches gently, not unpleasantly. My hands are hot in my tight gloves but I am not allowed to take them off. The choir boys are doing an anthem. It is nice enough. All the Westchester girls have their chins raised watching them. They are mostly very good-looking little boys, their cheeks pink with the effort they are making. Neither they nor the older boys and men singers raise their eyes from the music, anyway not until now that the sermon has begun and they have arranged their voluminous black skirts and white cassocks. Now their eyes search the front row of girls and even back to us. Chessie opens her big red mouth and picks at her hair. The minister is working himself up into a monotony of sound. It is like flies buzzing. Every now and then he bangs the pulpit and I jump and wonder if he has got one. My room-mate slips a note into my hand.

"It's Rhinelander. Some Hopkins (school) boys must be here."

I slowly begin turning my head. Good! Fräulein sitting up straight is nevertheless asleep. I turn my head a little more and look past her. A boy with close blond hair and straight mouth looks me in the eye. He has been watching me all along. He does not smile or move. I feel a faint sickly pleasure and stare back. My room-mate gives me a violent pinch.

"Ass, do you want to get caught?"

"In the name of the Father and of the Son and of the Holy Ghost." Rhinelander is finished. Another hymn. Fräulein wakes up; looks about. We pile out. I look over people's heads. I get a glimpse of him very broad across the back. I am not hungry. Outside I feel better. I begin to think of the chicken and mashed potato, banana salad with chopped nuts and ice cream. There is Mr. Fitzhenry, one of our curates. There are three of them and Dr. Meiklejohn. They take turns leading us in chapel every morning. Mr. Fitzhenry is the best looking of the lot but they are all boring, I think. Some of the girls think Mr. Fitzhenry is just sweet. He always is embarrassed. He is young. Facing a hundred girls' impudent faces early in the morning and saying his prayers with them I suppose is what makes him embarrassed. He has a thin angular face and a sharp nose. His cheeks are always red as if he had just come in from outside and I am sure his nose is cold to the touch like a dog's. Sometimes the girls tease him. Once they made me do it. We were dashing around outside sniffing the air before chapel and Fitz came along up the walk. I was given a shove toward him. "Mr. Fitzhenry, look, my ring. It is broken. It hurts. It is pinching my finger." I deliberately shoved my hand into his, palm up, close to his face. I bent my head forward and we both stared into my hand. It is a nice hand, very narrow. The end of each finger is pink. I moved my hand in his and the ends of my fingers curled up and looked pretty and appealing. My hair is in my eyes. I am quite cool. As Fitz's face gets redder and there are titters from behind, I am very calm. "Please — it won't come off." "Hold still, I have a little file in my knife." The chapel bell has rung but Fitz takes out his little file and files off my ring. "It is hot, you will set my hand on fire." As the ring drops to his other hand, he raises his head, which I have been considering boldly. I have absolutely no interest in him. We have been standing very close together which he seems suddenly to realize. "Here," he says. "No keep it," I say, and kicking up my heels I run as fast as I can to join the whole school waiting in the hall; giggling and whispering. He has avoided my eyes ever since. I wonder if he kept my ring.

Quiet Hour this afternoon and Victorine next door has got permission to study with my room-mate. But my room-mate has a sudden caller from home and Victorine will have to put up with me. She is older than I and very pale and pretty. She is restless and jumpy. She and my room-mate and the girl from Des Moines and Chessie Brooks get together afternoons in our room when I am out. When I come in they always stop talking and look at one another; one of them is apt to jump up and leave. My room-mate says I wouldn't be interested. Victorine wants to read to me. She walks around the room kicking at the rug. She wanted to talk to my room-mate. I sit down hard on the bed and watch her. She puts her mouth to the window and breathes faintly on it. A little patch of foggy haze results. She places her full lips to the spot gently and then quickly. Her hands are on her hips. She stands quietly, her mouth clinging to the cold pane. I am amazed at her behavior. "Victorine, what in the world." She turns quickly and laughs at me. Her lids have dropped partly over her eyes which gives her a strange indolent look. She brings the book over to my bed and stretches herself out beside me crossways, both our backs to the wall. One slipper drops off with a thump and she begins idly turning the pages. The story is not very good, in fact I am not listening. I don't like to be read to. Victorine stops and begins stroking my hair. I don't mind. She is very pale and smiling. For a long time she fingers my head and pulls gently at my hair. I like it. She has not said anything and neither have I. She puts her cheek quietly to mine and we stay this way. The door springs open quickly and Victorine is as quickly on her feet. "Hello!" "Hello!" My room-mate and she greet each other. Victorine begins to talk fast. "We were reading." I have not bothered to get up and I have a sudden thumping headache. My room-mate puts on the light and stares at me for a minute. Victorine picks up her shoe and runs off to dress for dinner. "How do you like Victorine? I bet you got a lot of studying done." "I feel sick." "What's the matter?" "I don't know."

*Chapter Seven*

I AM TERRIBLY
sick. My head aches rhythmically and hard. The shape of my
eyeballs is outlined in pain. I lie intensely still on my back. A cold
wet cloth over my eyes drips into my ears. I can hear the nurse
moving about in her starched clothes. "It will be better," she
says. Chicken pox. Dr. Brady knew it right away. My chest and
back are bright red and my forehead, even my nose. I am in the
infirmary which is at the top of the stairs, alone except for the
nurse. I can hear the girls run madly up the stairs at noon for the
mail and down again talking loudly for lunch. I have had a note
and some flowers from my room-mate. Fredericka too has sent
me pink carnations. Miss James has come to the door once and

smiled at me. "Poor little Georgiana." I smiled back. "There is one horrid little pox on the tip of your nose," she said. "I will write your Aunt that you are a good patient."

Dr. Brady is our school doctor. My sister hates him thoroughly. She was nearly fired from school last year because she would not allow him in the room when she was sick. She and Jean say that he doesn't know anything and that the only reason he is our doctor is that Miss James is in love with him. Every time he comes he goes into Miss James's room for a long time. I don't mind him very much and am polite to him. The first week at school there were schedules and he examined every one of us, one at a time in Mrs. Sterne's room. She sat in a chair and chaperoned. I stood and he sat facing me. He put his hands on each side of me and held his head to my side. He spread his knees so I could come closer. I stood still scarcely breathing. "Good," he said, "now skip; run down the hall fast to the end and back here to me." This was fun. I dash out. I knew study hall was going on below me. I came down as hard as I could in my rubber-soled shoes as I fled down the hall and back in record time. The whole place shook; probably below little bits of plaster fell on upturned faces. I ran up to Dr. Brady and resumed my position in front of him, docile as a pony. I laughed at him. He has a shaven head like a German and pale blue eyes. He places his head hard against me again, hurting my breast a little and with the pressure I feel my heart racing steadily: thump, thump, thump. I lean back from him a little and look at Mrs. Sterne. She is English and will give me some tea as soon as the doctor has gone. He puts a finger under my chin, smiles at me and says, "You'll do. Try not to be so strenuous. Take it easy." Here he is again in the infirmary. He seems very big today and carries a little bag. He grins at me; he really is quite nice. I wonder if he is in love with Miss James. He is handsome but she is white and stern with big black eyes and too fat. My head still aches badly and I don't want to move my eyes. He draws up a chair and runs his big hand down my arm to my wrist and the pulse becomes evident to us both. The nurse pats at the bed and says, "Yes doctor," and "No doctor." He doesn't look at her. Pretty soon he has gone, leaving advice of tablets. Has he gone to Miss James's study? Will he kiss her? How horrid. I cannot bear it and squirm and flop over on my side. The nurse looks over from her chair by the window. "Shall I read to you?" "No. Please will you put out the light? My eyes hurt." "I will get you something cool to drink." She goes out and the glass in the door shakes a little. When I am alone I remember Victorine at the window, her eyes closed and her mouth to the pane. I vaguely recall her stroking my hair and don't want to see her again. My heart beating a little fast; I place the inside of my two fingers along my mouth. They are dry and I wet them a little with my tongue. The pressure of my fingers and my mouth is like a kiss and it might be the boy I saw at church. But I would never kiss him, never really, no. Kissing was not to be endured ever. The nurse returns and finds me depressed. It is a nasty disease.

Finally I am allowed to sit up. I have lots of flowers and heaps of notes. My spots are gone and there is faint color along my cheekbones, unusual for me. I feel clean again. I have learned to endure a bath in bed. I don't mind any more the vague, gentle hands of my nurse constantly washing me in sections. She is terribly stupid. My lips curl at her stupidity. She is leaving. I have given her things, even some old fudge. She is so stupid. This morning I sat looking out of the window. In the back yard of our school is a small school for boys. Kids. Their bicycles are piled against the wall. I can see in the window. There is only one teacher and about a dozen boys. They are all younger than me. They can see me sitting here and they grin at me sometimes. The master looks around and stares at me too. There is a blond boy; I don't believe he is fourteen but I like him, just a baby like that. He wears knickerbockers but he is tall. He is thin. He watches till the others have gone along home and waits, straddling his bike, looking up at me. His face is serious and interested. "What's the matter?" "Oh, chicken pox — awful." "I'll bring you some chocolate." He rides away looking back and up to me. Now he brings me Hershey bars, flat and bent from the warmth of his hands. I let down a string and he ties them on. I can feel his hands and I jerk the string a little and he laughs. We are very intent. I don't eat the chocolate but put it away in a drawer. I like him and he watches me.

*Chapter Eight*

I AM GLAD I AM well again. The day I came out of the infirmary Victorine went up. She is much sicker than I was. Lying together like that on the bed, of course I gave it to her. My room-mate thinks it's funny. I am behind in my lessons but it is just a matter of borrowing notebooks. Mam'selle is sweet to me in class. "Little one," she calls me. Her dress is brilliant blue and her breasts wide apart. She opens the window in class and sniffs the air like a horse. Fräulein is awful. There are only eight girls taking German. We sit in a row in front of her and torment her. She is so ugly. Her face is white and fierce. She hates us. My eyes shine and I deliberately mispronounce the words and my translation is abominable. The others are delighted with me and in their small way bravely mimic me. Fräulein turns over and over a brass paper cutter in her hands and tries to control herself. She really hates us. Two girls are sitting back two rows behind us; they suddenly draw Fräulein's wrath. She taps her foot angrily, gripping the desk, her knuckles white, she gives it to them instead of me. I turn and look; they sit arm in arm, short-sleeved. One is the pale profile-faced, skimpy-haired Pauline, minister's daughter; the other Fredericka's older sister Martha who blushes at nothing and has big feet and hands and none of Fredericka's appeal. They are frightened at Fräulein's sudden attack. She is furious. "Disgusting — disgusting filthy girls. It is indecent. Unlink your arms!" I don't get it and am deeply interested. After class I catch up with Roberta. "What was it that made Fräulein so hellish mad?" Roberta put up her chin and laughed. "My dear, those two were stroking each other's arms. I don't know why Fräulein got so awful mad. It's nice. I love it. Pauline can do it best of all. I give her fudge for it. By the hour, my dear; it tickles." My next class is English. Ordinarily a cinch, I am stumped: Miss McCormick has a new idea. She makes us describe sounds. I chew my pencil to bits trying to think how an oarlock sounds when rowing a boat. Gosh. Really. I grew up in a rowboat. I rowed between my nurse's knees on one of the ponds on my grand-father's place. I can hear the oarlock still but how to make Miss McCormick hear it, I don't know. I prefer Burke's *Conciliation*. I don't know what it means but the "proposition is peace" is wonderful. Miss McCormick is pretty bad. She cries in class if her feelings are hurt. She is always on the verge of tears and makes us feel like brutes. She has vague blue eyes and crinkly thin hair. She is almost bald. She is young. She is supposed to write stories. She says we must respect her. She says I ought to write. Once she wrote across one of my themes, "shows great feeling." It was about the moon coming up. It was lousy.

Recess. We scramble out without hats or coats and run around in circles. I yip like an Indian, turn my ankle and yell with pain.

Fredericka throws long arms around me and squeezes me hard. "Darling, dance with me tonight, say yes." "Yes, yes, but I am dying – my ankle, oh." Fredericka is on her knees in the gravel rubbing it viciously. I feel faint with pain but it is soon over. I grab Fredericka's flat bangs and pull her to her feet. "Get me your sister's notebook. I want her outline on 'Comus.' I was sick when we had Milton. 'L'Allegro' is awful." We minced up the steps and down the hall singing loudly, "Come and trip it as you go, on the light fantastic toe – and in thy right hand bring with thee the mountain nimp sweet liberty." Lousy poet, Milton.

I just realized that Frances Wells was fired out of school. I noticed that she wasn't around but I thought she went home for a week end. I didn't like her much. She had a crush on Spencer, a day girl. She was crazy about her. Spencer is a good egg. She has a flat mouth like a boy's. She doesn't ever say anything much. She is shy and sandy-haired. I suppose she is homely. She walks down the aisle with straight shoulders. Frances was always after her and used to go home to her house when she could get permission, and Spencer stayed here with her a few times when Frances' room-mate was away. They were different from the others who have crushes, because they are the same age. Lots of the young brats have crushes on the older girls whom they don't get to see much. They just write silly notes and send them flowers. The older girls laugh at them mostly. Vera used to be so homesick it was disgusting. She's a foolish, effeminate little thing anyway, and she adores Tony Page. Tony goes into her room once in a while as a great treat and tries to comfort her. Vera gets a big thrill out of that and comes down to dinner looking like a doll with big round eyes. She's so little she's foolish. She gets positively weak if Tony speaks to her. After dinner she gets excused from study hour somehow and goes up to her room and writes in her journal. It must be sickening. She really is awful. She is the only girl in school taking Greek. Tony is all right. She lives in the best corner room in school with Governor Anderson's daughter. She is pretty but her face is too long and heavy at the bottom. She is very long in the waist with short legs. Her hair is yellow and has curly ends that get in her face. I don't know how she puts up with Vera. But at least they aren't friends at all. Frances and Spencer really were. They were always together and Frances didn't know anyone else at all. Frances looked like a servant. She had too much color in her cheeks and her hair was black and curled too much. Once or twice she stopped me in the hall. She lives at the very end of our hall but I don't remember about it much. I do remember one night I was bored and wanted to have some fun and I sneaked past Fräulein's door and ran fast down the hall in my bare feet. One dim light was shining and it was exciting. As I reached the end of the hall I heard Fräulein's doorknob turn. My heart stood still. I didn't dare barge in on Mary Susan who roomed opposite so I quickly opened Frances' door and crept in silent as a fog. "Shut up," I said. I slid under one of the beds and waited. Nothing happened. Only a whispering in Frances' bed. I crawled half out on my elbows and tried to see in the dark. Two heads on the white pillow. No one in the bed I was under at all. I recognized Spencer. "Hello," I said, "I didn't know you were here." Pat sat up. "Don't," said Frances. "Well," I said, "I only came for the fun of it, so long." I opened the door gently and sped back along the dim hall into my own room. I went up to my roommate. She lay with her face turned up into a light that shone in from outside. I felt depressed. Our room joins by a closet with Victorine's and Lenore's. I stepped along over shoes with dresses trailing me in the face. I opened the door and looked in. Both beds were empty. Disappointed I returned and slid into bed. My room-mate said, "For God's sake, shut up." I said, "This is the dullest school I've ever been in." After that I went to sleep.

*Chapter Nine*

ALK OF FRANCES.
No one seems to remember anything at all about her. No one knows what she did or why she was expelled. This morning after chapel when Miss James was calling the roll as usual and looking around the room at each name; "Middleton, F." "Yes, Miss James." "Middleton, M." "Yes, Miss James." She came to Wells and forgot. "Wells, F." There was a tense silence and Miss James bent down and crossed out her name. We heard the pencil point snap. "Zaslawski, L." "Yes, Miss James." Laura Z. is a girl six feet high. She stoops a little and has a lot of red hair and a long nose and small blue eyes. She always has books under her arm and says "What?" when you speak to her. Everyone turned and

looked at her today. The bell rang and we scattered to class talking loudly. The fact that Frances is gone reminds us all of the girl from Jacksonville, Florida. No one knew her very well either. I did not even know her name. She was tall and mature and used to swing her hips. I don't even remember her except from the back going down the corridor. She was quite beautiful. I don't remember her ever speaking to anyone. She disappeared after two weeks.

Of course, why Frieda isn't fired, no one knows. She's been caught again and again. I never did get my five dollars back. And Brooks went in her room when she was in class and found two of her best crepe de Chine chemises hanging up to dry by Frieda's radiator. Brooks's name is written all over them. How Frieda has the nerve, I don't know. She has an impudent small face and denies everything.

Her eyes are round and green with black eye-lashes equally long and curling away from the eye, top and bottom. She has a nice figure, quite flat, and wears shirtwaists and a tight short skirt always. It shows her hard thighs. She is very attractive. She never is a bit clean. She's quite frankly dirty. She says her body is covered with scars. My room-mate says it's true; anyone can see them that's interested. Frieda points them out and tells how she got each one. My room-mate says it's different every time. The girls would like to know really how she got them. My room-mate says she looks as though she had been through a meat chopper. Some of the older girls have tried to reform her, but she relapses almost immediately. Even Jean. Jean who is pink and fastidious and walks along on her toes. She wears embroidered smocks with some skirt and delicate legs showing underneath. She is my sister's room-mate and calls me a brat and says I am fresh. I think she is a deceitful little liar but she is pretty and I watch her. She tried to reform Frieda once. It lasted two or three days. Frieda sat beside her, my room-mate says, and kept her eyes down, the corners of her mouth up. When Jean had finished and said, "Frieda, really for your own sake," and touched her arm, Frieda raised her extraordinary eyes. "Jeanie, look." She lifted her skirt to where her long thigh fitted into her side. Jean saw a diagonal scar eight inches long. "My brother and I were out in our motorboat. He pushed me into the engine. I have another one on my tail. I was unconscious for two days. My grandfather beat my brother and the doctor sewed me up."

Frieda came out of her room this morning only the front of her face washed; buttoning on her shirt. "Come here," she said.

"What?"

"Something awful happened last night. I heard it. I heard a woman scream. She screamed and screamed. Something terrible happened to her."

I had a clear picture of a woman in her nightgown fleeing along the sidewalk, her mouth wide open, a black hole. I shivered. I hopped down the stairs to breakfast and watched Frieda, her head bent as Miss James returned thanks. I am sitting at Miss James's table now. It is supposed to be an honor. We are changed around every two weeks. Sometimes we beg to sit next to each other but Miss James sorts us all up so that we sit next to girls we don't like. I've got Louisa on one side of me and Teresa on the other. I am beginning to like Teresa. She plays the piano to me between study hour at night and go-to-bed bell. Her hands are quick and hard and beautiful. But Louisa is a little boob. She is white-blond and skimpy and ugly. She twitches her shoulder and drops her lip down over her teeth when she smiles so as not to look too damned pleased with herself. She was sent away to boarding school because she had too many beaux. So she says. The great hulk Rosa sits at the foot of the table opposite Miss James. She is so ugly I don't want to look at her but she is a favorite of Miss James. She is terribly cross-eyed. She weighs two hundred and forty pounds. She has big heavy shoulders and no neck. She goes along at a terrible pace in men's shoes. She likes to get a lot of us around her in the upstairs hall and exploit her ugliness. She makes frightful faces and she does a stunt which means she is an escaping criminal. She hangs along the wall; her big hands flat and outstretched and pretends to be getting away. She fascinates and scares some of the girls. She recites poems about eating worms, slippery ones and a woolly one, and makes faces to go with it. The girls scream with laughter and she goes on and on, making herself hideous. One night she said for us to come and she would hypnotize one of us. She picked out Janie and began to make passes at her and come up close to her and look her in the eyes. Janie began to get red in the face and giggle and Rosa told her she would have to be serious. Janie stood it for a minute or two and then began to scream. She screamed and began to cry and wring her hands and said, "Take her away from me." We all got frightened and Rosa stopped but Janie kept on screaming and started to laugh too. We made her go to her room and Mrs. Sterne gave her about a gallon of spirits of ammonia before she quieted down. My room-mate says Rosa ought to be shot.

After breakfast we run outside and walk fast arm in arm around the big asphalt circle in front of school before chapel. There is a high iron fence and we are not allowed to go outside it. Passers-by stop and stare. Men make remarks sometimes and we hear, "Girlie," and "The dark one." We don't look at them. We never get outside the schoolyard without a teacher or in groups to the corner to have a soda or a double banana split. Flower Seymour, a day girl, lives in the same block and I may go there sometimes. When I go, we steal her father's cigarettes and she tells the cook to have frozen pudding. I get very dizzy inhaling and it is pleasant. We both scrub ourselves in the bathroom and spray ourselves with perfume before I dare to go back to school. Today I found Brooks and the girl from Des Moines sprawling on my bed, and my room-mate. They were eating oranges and were excited and talking loud. There was a sign on the door saying, "No callers," but I went in, it being my own room. They stopped talking and looked at me. My room-mate got up and came to me. She smelled my jacket, "Oh, oh," she said. I said, "Can you really smell it?" And they all laughed and said, "You bad thing, you." Brooks went out. She had on bedroom slippers and big holes in her stocking heels. She said, "I'll tell you about Larry some other time. He's a devil." I began to take off my clothes and sniff at myself. My hair smelt like burning leaves and I took it down and brushed it hard. It sputtered and jumped and the girl from Des Moines said, "You ought to be a dancer because your skin is just the right color." I had on only a tight little brassiere and short silk panties. I was pleased and began to dance around with my hair flying. I lifted up my legs and bent my elbows. My room-mate said, "You're crazy."

Chapter Ten

THERE'S SNOW
and it's great fun. There's a steep little hill in the backyard and we
have permission to slide out the back gate and down Kenyon
Street almost into town on condition that we speak to no one
and walk back quickly. We wear shorts and sweaters. Mine
comes up high to my chin and I have woolen socks and galoshes.
I go on my stomach, preferably alone, and hold my legs high.
The turn through the gate is difficult but down the hill between
the trolley tracks is straight and swift. I yell with excitement
with Fredericka just behind me on her sled screaming, "Get out
of the way," and my room-mate just ahead of me hollering,
"A car! Look out you'll be killed." Well, anyway we can't ever

have such fun again because an old lady called up Miss James and said it was disgusting. Miss James gave a little speech after prayers saying she was sorry, she would like us to have healthy sport but the town was old-fashioned and girls in shorts with long legs would not be tolerated and besides we might be killed. There is lots to do lately. I am in a French play and the big play to come off just before Christmas. Mam'selle is very strict at rehearsals and so is Miss McCormick. In Mam'selle's play I say, "*Vive Henri Quatre. Vive le roi,*" and I sing a little song in a high clear voice. Sometimes I am on the key. I am a boy. I wear short tight pants and a page's hat. Mam'selle is pleased with me and says, "*bien, bien,*" and "*bon*" and "*bon.*" I sit beside her straddling my legs while the others are on. She turns her big bright eyes on me and we stare at each other smiling. She is cold and wears a little fur coat. The English play is not so easy. It is *The Importance of Being Earnest.* Miss McCormick is very serious and we work hard. I am Earnest. This is dress rehearsal and I wear my men's clothes for the first time. The footlights have been put in and the faculty is invited. We are made up and I smell the ether. Miss McCormick is nervous. I have two bath towels wrapped around me between my breasts and my hips. I am very slim and straight but this space must be padded to make me straighter. It is hot. I have on a dinner coat belonging to Mr. Fitzhenry. I try to remember him but it doesn't smell of anything, just a clothy smell. It fits me perfectly and I like to bend my knees and watch the crease come and go in my pants. The high stiff collar feels pleasantly tight around my neck. My hair is brushed back straight and in a flat braid disappears under my collar. My hands look small and frail and my feet look silly; otherwise I am perfect. I was very popular on the way down-stairs from my room. I had my hands in my pockets as I walked. The girls laughed and hung around me. Fredericka kissed my cheek and said, "I hate you as a boy" but Louise boldly put her arms around my waist and hugged me. She tried to kiss me but I gave her a push. The rehearsal went off very well. I was excited. Miss McCormick was pleased. The faculty clapped, even Fräulein; and Mam'selle did not take her eyes off me. Afterwards she took my chin in her hands and laughed in my face. I went upstairs three at a time and found Victorine and Lenore sitting around looking bored. "Pull up the shade," I said, "and we'll have some fun. Turn on all the lights. Oh! oh! the old ladies will be calling up by the dozen." Victorine said, "What do you want?" I said, "Put your arms around my neck. Take off your dress." Victorine nimbly stepped out of her clothes; little in her single slip. She quickly put her cheek up to mine and leaned against me. I was intent and bent my head to kiss her. She moved her hands up the back of my head. Lenore watched us. "You look real," she said. I gave Victorine a shove. "I guess they've seen us," I said. I pulled down the shade. "Pull off these pants. I don't see how Fitz can stand them. I'm hungry. I wish vacation were here and I could go home. I want to go skating."

*Chapter Eleven*

E CAME HOME
yesterday. Caroline and I. Page's eyelashes are longer than ever
from the side and there is bright color on his cheekbones. His
puttees are a little worn at the calves. He must interfere like a
horse. Grandpère and aunt greet us. Grandmère is somewhere
in the background. "Where is Bonny?" I say.

"Oh poor little Bonny has passed away."

"What do you mean? How?"

"We won't go into details," says aunt. "Poor little Bonny;
she didn't know; it was all so painless."

"Tell me," I say coldly, and I stare at my aunt.

"Come, come little girl take off your wraps," says my grandfather. "We had to have her chloroformed. She was getting old.
She suffered with age," says my aunt.

"Oh," I said, "Oh oh." I look with fury at my aunt. "Oh how really cruel." Then I went up to my room and cried. I cried for a long time. Every time I stopped I saw poor little tan Bonny with big beseeching eyes. If I had been here they would not have dared. Bonny is dead. Dinner wasn't very cheerful. I put my hair up and was frowned on for that except by grandmère: "She looks pretty," she said. Grandpère stepped to the sideboard and chose slowly a tall bottle of French Vermouth and one of Italian, and a square blue bottle. He slowly poured out his one cocktail. A little slice of lemon lay ready; he took a bit of the peel, ran it around the rim of the tiny glass and dropped it in. No one else was offered any. Grandpère's eyes are blue and the lids get a little pink after his one cocktail. Grandmère says, "Why don't you have another, Jasper?" And he says, "I don't want to form any bad habits." Grandpère can be gentle when he isn't in a temper. He calls grandmère "Effie" and sometimes at Christmas they waltz together and he kisses her under the mistletoe. She was very beautiful, he tells us, and he disappears and comes back down the stairs with a little bright daguerreotype which has not faded. It has a red plush cover and gold clasp. Inside is a plain little girl but she has a long lovely neck and enormous dark eyes. Her dark hair is parted in the middle and brushed straight down to her shoulders unbraided and unwaved. She can't be more than fifteen. We all bend over it. Grandpère's hand trembles a little and tears come into his eyes.

"Is that really you, grandmère?" I say.

"Your grandpère was handsome too," she says, "He was the handsomest young man in Tewksbery."

"I saw her and I said, 'I am going to marry her," said grandpère.

"We've been happy together," said grandmère, gallantly it seemed.

Grandpère went off and got his book; grandmère began to knit. Caroline comes down with pink cheeks. She has on a green felt hat and a green wool dress and her high-heeled pumps. Grandpère looks up.

"Where are you going?"

"To the movies."

"With whom, may I ask?"

"Kenneth. Please let me go."

"No!"

"Oh please. It's only the movies. Please."

Grandpère is furious. "No!"

The pink leaves Caroline's face and she is suddenly furious, too. We are all watching. I am frightened. Caroline's eyes get cold and hard and so do my grandfather's.

"I want to know why I can't go."

"Don't catechize me!"

"I want a reason."

"Reason enough — I said 'No!'" Grandpère's hand comes down hard on the open book.

"That is not a reason."

Grandpère is on his feet.

"Jasper!" says Grandmère.

Grandpère is trembling; his lips are white. Caroline stands defiant. She looks beautiful. Grandpère raises his arm and lets it fall, raises it again, and points to the stairs. "Go to your room. Stay there."

Caroline turns, first giving grandpère a long look and walks upstairs. Grandpère begins to walk up and down. "That young cub! Daring to come here with a cigarette in his mouth!" I start to get up.

"Stay where you are!" Having called his attention to me, he looks at me. "I suppose you will be gadding around next."

"Caroline doesn't gad around, Jasper."

"You keep out of this, Effie."

Later tonight when everyone is asleep, everyone but Caroline who has a shade over her light and is reading, I sneak out of bed and down the hall to grandmère's room. I slip in and bend over her. She is sleeping quietly. I touch her on the arm and say, "Grand." She opens her eyes. "What is it?"

"Grandmère," I whisper, "Crispin wrote me a letter at school.

He invited me to go to the hockey game; the Princeton hockey game."

"You shall go."



"Good night, grandmère." As I go on back to my room I smell a familiar smell. Caroline is smoking. I would like to go in but I don't because of the quarrel. I have nothing to say. I go on into my own room. There is cold night air in my room and in the distance I hear the eleven o'clock train rushing through. I am asleep when I hear voices in Caroline's room and in the hall. The voices are high and bitter. Grandpère is scolding Caroline. I hear my aunt's voice and then Caroline's answering back. The smell of cigarettes is strong even in my room. He caught her. The voices grow quieter and finally it is still again. I hear Caroline's electric light switch out and the two windows slam up one after the other. I am shivering with cold.

The next morning I asked Caroline what happened. She said it was awful. She said, "I had to take a cigarette out of my memory book. It had paste on it, but I couldn't go to sleep. Grandpère came down the hall in his nightshirt and slippers. He was mad. The room was full of smoke. He shook. It really was terrible. He began to cry. He said I was bad. It really was awful. He made me promise. He said never to smoke again. He said a woman who would smoke would do anything. I said I would promise. I said I promise never to do it again. Aunt led him back down the hall. If only he would not look so pathetic. Gosh it was terrible. I cried. I was furious."

Skating is nice. There was a big moon and it was as light as day. The Simpsons took us. Crispin held my ankles firmly between his knees and laced my shoes. His teeth were shiny in the light. He talks like an Englishman. He is already smaller than I am. I prefer to skate with Allyn. He looks down at me and holds me close to him. He is as hard as a post. I skate better than Caroline but we all skate well and fast. There are only a few others on the pond and their voices are clear. It is so still. The ice is black and thin. It cracks in tiny lace-like cracks under us and I scream at Allyn and Caroline to go away. I laugh with pleasure as we stop striking out and glide along fast, the ice so thin that it is swaying under us.

"Allyn," I call.

"Yes Georgie."

"It's wonderful." He puts his face down and opens his mouth at me and his hard white teeth are all I can see. Caroline is calling, "Come back, you idiots." But we know we can't stop or turn around or take a step. We would certainly go through if we did. Allyn is holding me tight and the moon shines up from the bottom of the lake. All of a sudden Allyn says, "Watch out," and we land in a heap on the side of the pond on the frozen grass.

"Please let's do it again. We'll go back and do it again."

"Next time we'll drown."

"Oh but I love it."

My feet are so cold that I cry all the way home and Allyn has to carry me in and deposit me on the sofa. "I wish we could ask you to stay and scramble some eggs," says Caroline, "but Grand-père would have a fit." She is very pink. Allyn is steaming like a horse. Crispin is looking down at me and saying, "Don't cry. Let me take off your stockings, I'll rub your toes, it's the only way, do let me, Georgiana."

"No, no."

There is a creaking of stairs and Aunt appears on the landing. Her eyes are blazing.

"Good night, Allyn. Good night, Crispin. Caroline and Georgiana, it is eleven o'clock."

There is an embarrassed grabbing for caps.

"It's sickening," says Caroline as we go upstairs to bed. "Simply disgusting and unbelievable. I think I'll get married."

I look at her in frightened admiration.

"To whom?"

"Oh Stephan. I suppose he'll make a good husband but he's a fool."

"You'd better not," I say wisely. "It'll be worse."

"It couldn't be worse. It's sickening. Being put to bed in broad daylight. It's really awful."

$\mathcal{I}$ MUST ADMIT IT'S a good thing we are going back to school soon. Even Christmas day was ruined. Everything was all right until the express man arrived about three in the afternoon with a big package for Caroline. The horse clattered up the street and drove in the dirt road to the side door. We all ran to the window. "Gosh," I said, "if it's a barrel of chocolates I'll be sick. I'll up-chuck." The top of the piano is covered with five-pound boxes — from Stephan and Kenneth and Allyn and Crispin and Reg. But this looks more interesting. The express man brings it in. Grandpère gives him a Christmas gold piece and he grins and salutes. "Merry Christmas, Mr. Lord, Sir."

It has to be opened properly and grandpère does it deftly and neatly and slowly. A card slips out. "Merry Christmas to Caroline from Peter Brandon." I anticipate trouble. In the first place, it's Peter, and in the second place, it's not chocolates or flowers. Good Lord, it's golf clubs! the most beautiful and complete set and the bag with C.P.L. The brassie shines and the irons look like platinum. The straight wooden shafts are delicate and fair. Caroline pulls one out, straddles her legs, and drops the head of the club gently to the rug. She has been getting along with a pretty rotten set of moth-eaten clubs. The first words come from aunt and they are cold.

"The Brandons. Mustard!"

Caroline goes on wiggling and getting a good stance.

"You will send them back at once."

"How wicked," I say, suddenly hot. My impertinence is not noticed as Aunt continues. "You planned this present with him."

"I did not."

"Don't contradict your aunt."

"I did not ask for them. He saw what lousy clubs I had in the fall. I can't send them back. It would be rude and awful."

"He will perhaps learn that he cannot treat my niece as if she were a common person."

"Common. Hell!"

"Caroline!"

"But grandpère, please let me keep them. He's a nice boy; he's very sensitive. I can't send them back."

"His father makes mustard and I have never called on his mother."

"Grandpère."

"Do as your aunt says. She is doing it for your own good."

Caroline drops the club and makes for the stairs. There is the slam of her door at the end of the hall. I take a deep breath and smell nothing but Christmas tree. I come back into the room and sit on a window seat and admire it. It is wonderful. My heart is beating fast from the quarrel; always a succession of quarrels about things. Last summer that time that Mr. Wagstaff drove up in his Mercer and said, "Here look what I've caught for you." He had on white duck trousers and he held up a shining bluefish. Caroline wasn't much impressed with the fish but she looked with admiration at Mr. Wagstaff who was twice her age, and a member of a sophisticated group, no one of whom had scarcely spoken to her before. "Pretty thing, what?" he said. He turned the fish about; it had a great glazed eye. Caroline laughed. "Suppose I give it to your cook, what; here, let's go." He stepped out and we went around to the side with him. "Look here, will you come with me tomorrow on the bay? Nice little ship I've got. My sister will come along."

"Oh I'm sorry. I'm awfully sorry. I can't. You see."

"What?"

"I can't."

Mr. Wagstaff looked unhappy. "I say, I'm sorry too. So long. You'll let me look at you at the club I hope. Beautiful swing you've got. Well. Good-bye."

My word, the scene that took place five minutes later. Aunt said she had known the Wagstaffs a long time and Jim Wagstaff was notorious. He belonged to a very fast set and it was an insult to Caroline for him to dare ask her to go anywhere with him. I don't remember if we sent back the fish but we've not seen Mr. Wagstaff since.

BACK AT SCHOOL and there's a new girl from England. I like her at once. She's homely with a face like a horse and big wrists. Her hands are red as if she had been washing dishes but she talks more like a lady than any of us. She says she likes me better than anyone. She made me write "hello" on the bottom of a letter she wrote to a boy she likes in England. Her name is Mabel. The boy's picture is pinned on the wall. I stare and stare at him. All the girls come in and take a look. He is beautiful like a girl with fair straight hair and undoubtedly blue eyes. His mouth dips gently down. He looks like a little man, nevertheless. The girls study his face and then look at Mabel without any attempt to hide their puzzlement. "But he's too sweet." "Mabel, do ask him to our dance in June." Brooks actually leers at the poor boy, sticking out her underlip, but she turns away and shrugs her fat shoulders. "Looks like mama's boy to me. I like 'um sophisticated." Gaining an audience she wets her finger and sticks a wisp of hair on her cheek into a curve. "Larry says I'm Spanish." She wiggles her hips and the backs of her knees show. "He says I'm hot-tempered." She giggled. "Maybe we didn't have fun vacation. Of course Larry's no kid. He's twenty-two. He can't wait to marry me." A senior girl stuck her head in the door. "Oh shut up, Brooks." She looked at me, "You run along, babe in the woods. Brooks is a big liar." Brooks grew red to the hairline. "Jealous," she said when the senior had gone on down the hall, "Filthy jealous. She couldn't make Larry herself if she tried." Passing out the door with her arm around the girl from Des Moines she poked at me, "Sweet sixteen and never been kissed."

"I'm fifteen."

She took no more notice of me and began to whisper with wet lips into the girl's ear. Halfway down the hall we heard them burst into hilarious laughter. The girl from Des Moines came back from vacation with a ring, a real diamond on her engagement finger. Her room is full of roses and she gets special delivery letters by the dozen. My room-mate says she bought the ring herself and sends herself the flowers. She's always talking about Jimmy. He goes to Yale. She says Miss James thinks he's lovely and that he can call every Sunday. My room-mate says she doesn't know what Miss James is up to. She lets the girl do anything she likes; she says the girl told her herself that she spent the week end in a hotel in New Haven with Jimmy and that Miss James knew it. I've seen him, so at least he exists. He doesn't look like the boys at home. He's got a waist. I wasn't supposed to see him. Sunday during quiet hour Fredericka jumped into my room. Her flat bangs were hanging in her eyes. She said "Sssssh" and flattened herself against the door; Fräulein's footsteps arriving outside, silence, and they went on. "Sneak," whispered Fredericka. "Look, let's have some fun. Jimmy is calling on Des Moines this afternoon. You and I will take a peek at him You have a front window. Let me know when he comes. So long I got algebra to do." My room-mate looked at me in disgust "Haven't you ever seen a man before."

"Not this one."

We both hung out the window. The cold air went down my blouse and I shivered. "Ouch," I said. "There he comes," said my room-mate. Leaning out we could see along the front of the building girls' heads sticking out. Even Tony, in the corner room and Governor Anderson's daughter were hanging out, balanced on their stomachs. Tony's hair was pulling away from her head and shining in the sun. Jimmy came up the walk pretending not to hear girlish giggles and even remarks passed from window to window, such as "Nice day, isn't it," and "That's what you think." He had on a grey hat and we could see his shoes shining Just before he climbed the steps he flicked away a cigarette. It spun through the air and landed on the lawn. We all laughed as if it were funny. He stood with his finger on the bell and we heard it through the house. Windows slammed. I jumped up and down with the cold and sniffled. My room-mate began pulling on her best clothes; going to Mam'selle's for tea. I wish I could go but I can't until I am a Junior. Mam'selle has an apartment a block away. She would not live at school for anything She wrinkles up her nose at the idea. She lacks respect. As we march in singing a hymn at chapel, Mam'selle, standing in a row with the others, winks at me and looks as though she would die laughing at me. Sometimes she looks at Miss James, solemn and black-eyed on the platform, and gives a little shrug and purse her mouth, wiggles her shoulders. I have to hide my face in my prayer book. The other teachers look solemn. Miss McCormick with watery sentimental eyes and soft thin mouth; Fräulein always disgusted and inwardly blazing with anger; Miss Haynes Latin since 1898, dim-eyed, singing off key in a wavering thin soprano. Mam'selle seems not to want to be a part of them and stands straight with her arms close to her side. She doesn't deign to hold a hymnal nor does she bow her head at the name of Christ or the Holy Ghost. She doesn't make the responses or say "and with thy Spirit." I am thrilled a little at her independence. She stares rudely around at the girls, at the pictures of Dante on the walls, and at the curate. My room-mate is off, her nose powdered dead white and bits of powder clinging to her lashes. "So long, Mam'selle will have little hot cheese things, oh boy." Quiet hour is over and there's a week day buzz. A long-legged girl is racing down the hall screaming with laughter. Short Pauline, the girl who was sent to school because she had so many beaux, is red in the face and stamping her foot. "Make her give me that letter." She appeals to no one in particular and no one pays any attention. Fredericka comes hopping along and we go into a huddle. "Which room will they be in?" I ask, doubtfully. "How can we possibly see?" "Oh I've watched lots of times," says Fredericka, her eyes shining. "My dear, it's an education. I know where they'll be. Come on. Don't look as if we were going anywhere." We walk slowly through the halls arm in arm until we reach the side stairs that are used for gym and showers but which also connect with Study Hall. No one in sight; we dash down and land at the bottom out of breath and excited. "There, in there," whispers Fredericka. "Get down, get down." We stoop down and tiptoe to the door with a glass top that leads to study hall. "We'll take turns; you look." I lift my head, trembling with excitement and look in. Across the hall in one of the back seats are Jimmy and Des Moines. He has her pushed back hard against the back of the desk, both of his arms are around her, his mouth is on hers and they are absolutely still. I am so shocked and horrified that I cannot move. Fredericka, who has been holding on to my knees, pulls me down; her eyes are enormous. "Didn't I tell you? Oh, oh, now it is my turn." I go away and sit on the bottom stair. My heart is beating in great slow hard beats. "Fredericka, let's go away from here." But Fredericka is all eyes. Her mouth is curved up, and now and then she says, "Oh, oh." Suddenly she ducks. At a sound inside we make a break up the stairs. Reaching the top we hang on to each other and wait. "I can feel your heart," whispers Fredericka. "Look!" Jimmy and Des Moines have come out in the hall. Oblivious of prying eyes they start hugging each other. "Good-bye, honey." Fredericka squeezes me so I can scarcely bear it. "Look!" she says again. "Watch." Jimmy lowers his hands and Des Moines arches back from his face. Her reddish hair is damp on her white forehead. Her mouth is drooping and her eyes are closed. "Good-bye, honey." I drag and pull at Fredericka. I feel worse at the repeated word, "Honey" than at the kissing. Fredericka finally gives in. "You make me sick. It's better than a movie. I saw him with his knees in there." "It's awful," I say. "I hate it."

"Don't tell."

"No."

"Cross your heart."

"Cross my heart."

# Chapter Fourteen

FLOWER SEYMOUR
is in tears part of the time and furious the rest. Her father is getting married again and she hates the woman. She says she'll surely leave home. I was there yesterday. Dr. Seymour is very good-looking. He has a short red pointed beard. He kissed me on the lips and his beard stung me. He said, "I am glad Flower has you for a friend. You will come often." F. glowered. I wondered if he missed his cigarettes and only yesterday we took his fine red claret out of the sideboard and made ourselves bitter lemonades and sucked our lips. His new wife is plump and young. She gives the impression of wanting to be chased. Dr. Seymour looks at her all the time and his eyes shine. He crosses one long

black leg over the other and while his wife talks he lifts his long narrow foot up and down slowly. The new wife wonders if Flower wouldn't like to board at the school and come home week ends. Flower says, "Daddy, Daddy," and leaves the room quickly. I don't know what to do.

"Run after her. Poor little girl, emotionally unstable like her mother," says Dr. Seymour, taking out a cigarette and tapping it nervously. The new wife spreads her hands and looks pretty and hurt.

"What have I done? I only meant. Why I thought she'd be pleased." She burst into tears. Dr. Seymour began to make soothing noises and took her in his arms. "My darling." "Oh, oh. Blub." My God, I thought and ran off after Flower. I found her on the bed, her head lowered. Things had been pretty much thrown around the room. A picture of her mother and father, in a double frame, lay face down on the floor. "Flower," I said, "for cripe's sake." I pulled up her head. "Flower!" She had sunk her teeth so deep into the flesh between thumb and forefinger that drops of blood decorated the edge of the bite and the flesh was pushed up white in the middle. The mark of each tooth showed plainly. As I stared, Flower lowered her head again and deliberately fitted her teeth to the impression they had left, and drawing away her lips began steadily biting. She looked me in the eye as she did it. "You must be crazy, stop it." Flower stopped and pulled up the sleeve of her blouse. "Look." Along her arm were a series of small bite-shaped scars. She was pleased with my astonished interest. "But this was the worst one here." She showed me scars not yet white on each side of the knuckle of one of her fingers. "Daddy had to bandage that one." "But Flower, why?"

"It was in English class. I did it in class. I did it because Miss McCormick doesn't like me. She's never liked me." At a knock on the door, Flower jumped and then called out rudely, "What do you want." The new Mrs. S. came in timidly, her eyes red and her mouth big from being kissed. "Flower, dear." Flower stared at her. "Flower, dear," she mimicked. Big tears started rolling down Mrs. S.'s round cheeks. "I'm going to kill myself," said Flower calmly.

"Flower, shut up," I said.

"I've tried and tried," whimpered Mrs. S. turning to me. "And Charles is the same. He didn't even come home for vacation."

I looked at the one remaining picture on the bureau. Mrs. S. followed my eyes and so did Flower's. All three looked at Charles' picture. Flower picked up a blue china bowl by her bed and let it drop. Mrs. S. fled. I told Flower I thought she was hateful and that her new mother couldn't help being a fool.

# Chapter Fifteen

*E*VERYTHING IS
very dull. We leave our windows open now and lean far out and
stare at passers-by. It smells good out and I am lazy. My legs ache.
My room-mate has a check for new spring clothes and a teacher
will go and see that she doesn't waste her money. I have never
been allowed to buy myself anything. I shall continue to wear
my wool dress. It is hot around my neck. We yawn all through
class and even the teachers begin to doze toward noon. Mam'selle
stands in a thin dress by the window and sniffs and shivers.
People look in from the street and we can just see their heads
over the sill. The chalk breaks and drops to the floor and Mam'-
selle leaves it there. Fräulein doesn't even keep order and the

girls loll and straddle and look sullen. Miss McCormick appeals to our better natures and begs us to remember that our parents are making sacrifices for us. She takes out her handkerchief and dabs at her eyes but no one takes an interest in Burke's *Conciliation*. I take pity on her and pull myself together, "I know it by heart, Miss McCormick." Her eyes light up. I stand and recite without hesitation the entire "proposition is peace" paragraph. I sing-song it; I haven't the slightest idea what it means. Miss McCormick is delighted. She puts ninety after my initials on a big white card. Fredericka sneers at me after class. "Since when did you become a filthy grind?" "Me a grind? I've never opened my Burke; I've heard the rest of you read it often enough in class; you're such dummies." Fredericka grabs me by the arms and sticks her pointed chin into my shoulder.

"Ow."

"You're the prettiest girl in school. Don't dance with anybody but me tonight."

After prayers we begin. René sits down at the piano and plays one jazz tune after another, one foot clamped on the loud pedal, the other going up and down in time to the music. A girl at the end of the room begins a variegated tap dance and black-bottom. She rolls her eyes and wags her head. She turns in her knees and flips up her heels. Her little silk dress with a high collar she lifts to her waist. She is very good and we begin to clap.

"That will be about enough," says Fräulein. "You are a little hoyden."

"I'm a hot mama."

"Go to your room." Fräulein is in a rage again. She turns on the rest of us. "You behave as if you were picked off the street. You are a disgrace to the school." No one said anything. She looked at me. "And you too. You — you are a wicked little thing." She left. We weren't impressed. René started in on a waltz. Fredericka and I are expert. We weave in and out among the clumsy ones close together; Fredericka's arm like an iron hand across my back, her long fingers entirely around my arm. We are the same height and we dance cheek to cheek. I am hot and panting when we finish. I have to pull my hair out of my ears. It it wet and I stick it behind my ears and take deep breaths at the window. "René, one more." "I'm pooped," says René. A chic figure appears in the door. Mary Susan back at last, ten days late. She looks about and doesn't smile at any of us. She has cold dark blue eyes with black lashes and brows. She has a small straight mouth and her chin sticks up. She has on a dark suit and a black fur. She has on sheer stockings and she hasn't taken off her gloves. "Where's Miss James?"

"Upstairs."

An older girl calls out, "Where the deuce have you been, Mary Susan?"

Mary Susan doesn't smile. "Home." Mary Susan has a cultivated way of speaking and makes the others seem like louts. She takes off her fur and lets it drag along the floor after her as she walks off and upstairs. A couple of seniors appear in the hall and begin talking together. Brooks calls out to Des Moines, "Come here, I have to tell you something." They go off and sit on the stairs. A freshman with straight yellow hair curving at the ends into her mouth says, "I think she's stunning." She appears again in the middle of study hour, walks down the senior aisle and begins rummaging in her desk. She takes out books and papers. A powder box drops out and rolls along the floor to the feet of the freshman girl. Everyone is watching. The freshman girl looks at it a minute and then reaches down and picks it up, slides out of her seat and hands it to Mary Susan. Mary Susan gives her a little smile and the girl blushes. No one makes a sound. Mary Susan goes on rummaging and finding what she wants, straightens up and clears out. There is a faint perfume. Brooks sniffs it loudly and Janie lets out a giggle. Fräulein at the desk says, "Two demerits for Carson and Brooks for giggling and disturbing study hall." All heads go down. Brooks says, "I didn't giggle." "You sniffed," said Fräulein, "and you may stand when you speak to me." Brooks stands up and flops down again

noisily, letting her eyes wander around for approval. There is
none. I loaf and watch the clock; the minute hand goes around
evenly, the big hour hand jumps convulsively and finally it is
nine o'clock. Everyone knows it except Martha in the back row
scribbling hard in her English notebook. She'll be there after we
all have gone. It is a minute past nine and Fräulein's head is still
bent over her book. I cough. She looks at the clock. "Study hall
is dismissed." I wander upstairs. I hear voices in Miss James's
study and instead of going straight up to the third floor, I stroll
by. Miss James is sitting at her desk and Mary Susan is standing
up. Miss Pinkerton is sitting up straight in a chair. She must have
just come; she still has on her traveling clothes. I am not very
curious and go on up to my room. My room-mate is writing a
letter and two juniors are straddling a wastebasket eating oranges
and dropping the skins in it. "Hello," I say. I feel I have news
though I am not sure what it is.

"Guess who is back."

"Oh, Mary Susan, we saw her."

"She's looking snootier than ever."

"Yes, but Miss Pinkerton has finally showed up."

"I told you so," said one of the juniors to the other.

My room-mate stopped writing. "She's got her nerve."

"If she had any brains or sense," said the second junior, "she'd
have at least waited till tomorrow."

"I was beginning to think they had both been fired," said my
room-mate.

"Fired," I said, "for what?"

"Oh not for much."

"Oh no, not very much."

"Oh noooo."

The second junior bit into another orange and looked at me
over the top of it. "Don't you know what's going on around
here, darling?"

"Mary Susan is a snob," I said, "but I wouldn't want her
fired."

"Neither would Pussy Pinkerton, you can bet."

"Mary Susan's family is rich as hell," says my room-mate. "She won't be fired. And besides there wouldn't be anyone to take the man's part in the senior play. Mary Susan is the only one without any hips. They'd have to get this gigolo here to do it." She points at me. After awhile the juniors leave and we go to bed.

"Hey," I say, "Why?"

"Oh nothing."

"But why fired?"

"Well everyone says they've been spending vacations together for three years. Mary Susan never speaks to anyone but Pinkerton and Pinkerton is a slimy cat. It's perfectly obvious. All the girls know it and I guess Miss James can't avoid a showdown this time. My God, they've stayed three weeks overtime. Do you *compree?*"

"Yes. I mean no."

"Well, good-night."

"Good-night."

# Chapter Sixteen

*T*HE FIRST THING
I notice in chapel next morning is that Miss Pinkerton isn't in
line with the faculty. I can see that Mary Susan is there, though,
in senior aisle and she looks clean and cool. At recess time when
we are allowed to dash up and buy pads or pencils, some of us
run up to see if Miss Pinkerton is there. But Miss McCormick is
there selling erasers and notebooks and having to follow a list of
prices. Her mouth is shut tight and she is not inclined to answer
any indirect questions. The bell for class rings before she has
been able to serve half the line and we run down pell-mell. I
nearly upset enormous Rosa on the stairs and cry, "Excuse it
please," at her not very politely. She is looking surly lately. She
could only make a certain number of faces and she doesn't excel
in anything else but size. We like each other pretty and Rosa is

ugly. Miss Wyman seems to be a friend of hers. Miss Wyman is on the faculty but we don't see her much. She has the junior school in the back room. Little day girls from town from six or eight up. She is so simple and sweet that I always feel like being disagreeable to her. She seldom speaks and when she does she blushes. Whatever for? She is young and a little fat. Her brown hair is woolly and her eyes wide but usually downcast. Her mouth opens and shuts in Chapel but not a sound comes out. She is the kind of person whose husband would beat her just for the pleasure of it and she would only look at him with big round eyes. She really is stupid. Rosa must feel superior with her; skipping along in her man's shoes and cross-eyed. Spring is really coming now and there are crocuses coming up. Flower digs them up and eats them like radishes. Which reminds me that Frieda eats butter on her celery. I am at her table now, supervised by Fräulein. Frieda eats the most enormous amounts of everything and doesn't gain an ounce. She is excited tonight and seems to challenge the table with marble blue eyes and curling lashes. She looks pretty but her neck is dirty. She wears a continuous curving smile. There is a great deal of noise at Miss McCormick's table. We all turn and look. Someone has the giggles and is suffocating with them. My room-mate is slapping her much too hard on the back and offering her a glass of water. Miss James taps with her fork on her glass and there is immediate silence. "The girl who is causing the disturbance may be excused." A tall girl scrapes back her chair and lopes out; her face very red. Miss McCormick looks mortified.

"Georgiana, eat your dinner," from Fräulein.

"I am, Fräulein."

I pretend to saw hard on my second joint of chicken. I pretend to give up and lay down my knife. The others are amused.

"Is your piece tough?"

"Oh no, Fräulein. It's very nice, it just won't relax."

I am delighted with myself for this remark and Frieda gives a guffaw. I am looking so politely at Fräulein that she has to overlook my impertinence. Frieda says, "Come up with me after study hour. I want to show you some snapshots of my little brother."

She's right beside me as the hour is dismissed and I have to go along with her. She has a little single room and it is stuffy and hot. I open the window and sit on the sill. Frieda's bureau is covered with photographs; lots of girls in cardboard folders, warped and slipping; some almost curled completely up, their faces contorted. There are odd pieces of silver. I have a horrid feeling they are not really hers. There are no pictures of her parents. There are several of a little boy growing up, one in his perambulator, one in his tricycle. Now he is five. He is pretty and appealing. Frieda holds the picture over to me.

"He is adorable," I say.

"He is precious," says Frieda, scrutinizing him closely herself. "He is the only one I love. Look, I am sending in a story about him. I got five dollars for the last one."

Frieda is always making a dollar here and there. She even knits things and takes them down to the woman's exchange. Of course it isn't allowed.

"His name is Jackie. Look, the story begins, 'Little Jackie was saying his prayers. . . .'"

"Frieda, that's very nice. Did he really say it?"

"Oh, yes." Frieda takes a large powder puff and runs it over her short nose and along the line of her chin and jaw. The dead white powder shows up the brown neck. She lifts her head and stares at it; wets her finger and rubs it. The blood leaves the place and then comes back hard leaving a red streak.

"That hateful Jean said for me to go wash my neck," said Frieda sticking out her lips. "I did wash it yesterday. It's not dirty. And besides," she turned her arc lights on me, "what I know about Jean." She looks at me significant of something untellable. "What I know about Jean. And Rosalie! What I know about Rosalie!" She lowers her voice and looks about. "She has been here three years and I know she has never had it." I feel something insulting has been said but I am unaware of its meaning. "Frieda, no." "Yes. Honest." "Georgiana, will you come and visit me after school? Please. Jackie is so sweet. I don't like any of the other girls and they don't like me." She looks as though she might cry. Her eyes are still wide open but a film comes over them like a dog before he finally closes his eyes and goes to sleep.

"Don't be silly."

"I am terribly afraid of my grandfather," says Frieda looking brighter.

"Afraid?"

"Uh huh."

"Of your grandfather?"

Frieda pulls her legs up under her on the bed and looks past me out the window. She looks inspired. She shakes her shoulders. "He's terrible. He's a terrible old man. Georgiana."

"What."

"You don't know how terrible my life has been."

"I'm sorry."

"They sent me here to get me away from my grandfather. I'm afraid if he finds out where I am."

"Frieda, I'm sorry, I have to go."

"No. Look, look what I have for you. A present. I want to give it to you." She jumped up and opened a drawer. She hunted around and pulled out a little lace collar. "Look — it's real lace — it's beautiful."

"You mustn't give it to me."

"Please keep it."

"Thank you very much."

"Georgiana, my grandfather took me to his room when I was fourteen. If I had been any older, I would have had a baby. He took me to his room and did it to me." She stood with her back to the door, straddling her legs, her hand on the knob. "There now, don't you tell."

"Oh, no." I held out the little rumpled lace collar. "It's too lovely. I mustn't take it."

"Yes, take it." She opened the door and let me go.

# Chapter Seventeen

NANCY B. IS A MIN-
ister's daughter and a junior. I didn't even know she was in school
until lately. Now she has taken to asking me to dance and it's a
nuisance. In the first place, she's fat. Fat and pale. Fat and brown
isn't so awful but Nancy B. looks as though she'd give easily to
a knife and only a sprinkling of blood would happen like sand.
She is a pie face and rolls her eyes back into her head. She is
embarrassed. I had to dance with her. She asked and asked. She
held on to me loosely and took little mincing steps frontward
and then backward. I begged Fredericka with my eyes but she
sulked against the wall and chewed the ends of her hair. Nancy

B. clapped and clapped for an encore and I looked at her with hatred but was too polite to run away.

"Fredericka," I called, but she turned away.

"Isn't it scrumptious," said Nancy B.

"You make me sick," I thought to myself. I saw Mam'selle standing in the doorway with a pencil in her hair. She caught my eye as I jigged by with Nancy. She put her hand up to her big grinning mouth and shook her shoulders up and down. Then she pointed to Nancy's rear and turning a little shook her own tantalizingly. I wasn't in the mood to admire her long thighs or her big fascinating feet with dusty old blue slippers on them. I hated Nancy B. who was staring at me with pale blue eyes and as gently as I could I pushed her away and stopped dancing.

"I got to study," I said. "It's study hour." We both looked at the clock. It was fifteen minutes till study hour. I said, "I've got a headache." Her hand was still on my waist. I straightened out her fingers and dropped her hand. "My head aches," I said. Mam'selle was loitering around the corner as I ran out of the room and put out her long brown hand with big knuckles and two big rings. She wrapped it around my arm where it bends at the elbow and laughed in my face. She smelled like a very cold geranium. As usual, I looked at the space between her breasts.

"You little miserable," she said, pinching my arm till I squirmed. "Why don't you cry. Go on — cry. That fat girl; ugh. Ooof, it is so funny. Go on. Go 'way." The bell rang five minutes early and Fredericka came along, a little contrite and put her long arm around my neck and we sauntered into study hall. How funny, Miss James is on the platform tonight. We slide into our seats and crash around in our desks. Miss James taps a little suspension bell on the desk and quiet is instantaneous. Her big black eyes are uncompromising tonight.

"Girls." We squirm. What have we done now. "Girls." The silence is broken by the skinny blond Louisa. She sneezes three times in quick succession and is hunting wildly for a handkerchief. "Girls. Last night in my absence there was disorder during study hour. Yes. Disorder. Considerable disorder. I expect the girl who caused the disorder to apologize. To apologize. The disturbance was very annoying to those who wished to study. I expect the girl who caused the disturbance to apologize to those girls who wished to study. Now." The silence following this little speech is quite sickening. I know at once that it is I. My cheeks are very hot; my heart begins to beat slow and hard. I feel at once the injustice of this scene in which I shall suffer. I know at once that Rosa has been telling tales. I am calmer and turn and look at her great hulk hovering over her desk in the back row. She drops her head.



"Georgiana."

"Yes, Miss James." I stand up shaking a little.

"You will apologize."

"No."

"You will apologize for disturbing the others."

"I didn't disturb them."

"You are contradicting me."

"I didn't disturb them."

"Georgiana."

"It was hot. I opened a window. Someone shut it. It got hot again. I opened the window. Someone shut it. I opened it. Someone shut it. I opened it — someone."

"That's enough. You will apologize."

"No."

I faced the school. "I disturbed none of you and you know it. If I disturbed you, I will apologize. You know I disturbed none of you. You liked it. It was fun. I disturbed none of you. Did I? Say so and I will apologize. Rosa. Did I by any chance disturb you?" Rosa's face got spotty red and Miss James became pale and furious.

"Sit down."

"Yes, Miss James."

"You will stay here in this study hall until you come to your senses."

"Miss James," I said, jumping up, "I will apologize to you. To you, because you seem to think I have insulted and disturbed you; but I have not disturbed the others, and I shall never apologize to them. It would be ridiculous. They are cowards or they would say so. Tell her," I said.

Nothing.

Suddenly the tears came to my eyes and the dominating figure of Miss James seemed to jump up and down on a horizon. The girls' heads looked like a lot of melons. No one spoke. The tears came faster and faster. My tears infuriated me.

"All right," I cried out, "all right, I apologize. I apologize for disturbing you. You hateful deceitful little mutts. Dirty little cowards."

Weak and terribly miserable, I got into my seat and let my head fall in my hands.

"Study hall is dismissed," said Miss James.

Well.

Mrs. Sterne brought some sickening aromatic spirits to my room and I drank it. She was grave and kind.

"You shouldn't," she said. I felt better. I sat up with pillows behind my back. I felt as if I had been to a dance. A note was shoved under my door.

"It is a shame, when we all need you so. Try to be calm." From Miss McCormick. A pretty good egg, after all. My room-mate stood by the window. She turned around, pale and sorrowful. "I hate all of us," she said, "especially me. Not to have had the nerve. Oh why didn't I stand up. If I only had. I feel like a pig."

"You couldn't," I said. "What's the use. I don't care. Only grandpère. She'll write home to him. Or worse, she won't. My card will just say 'Behavior: zero.' He'll think I committed adultery. Caroline got zero once. It was awful."

"If everybody was as good as you," said my room-mate intensely, "if everybody was as good as you and you're always in a mess. You've never even been kissed." She looked at me as if I were something funny. "Never even been kissed. My God, I've been kissed and kissed. Gee, I've been kissed. Thompson couldn't believe his ears. I told him you were one girl I know who couldn't be kissed. He said, 'Tell it to the Marines.' I got mad at him. I said, 'It's true.' He said, 'She's pretty as hell.' He said you were pretty as hell. I said, 'Of course she is.' I said, 'You make me sick. You think you can kiss anybody.' "

A timid repeated knock on the door and shadow of feet underneath made my room-mate shut up.

"Come in. Stick in your head," she hollered.

Miss Wyman appeared whole. She had been crying. She looked very pretty in a simple, stupid, dumb way. Her eyelids fluttered. She was pink all over and her bosom, which is all in one piece, went softly up and down. "May I come in?"

"Gosh, Miss Wyman, I'm sorry," said my room-mate.

"It's quite all right. Georgiana dear, I've come to tell you. I've come to tell you." She looked shy and frightened the way a *jeune fille* is supposed to look.

"Yes, Miss Wyman?"

"That you mustn't think that Rosa." She dropped her eyelids entirely, she might be asleep, "She is so upset. She is terribly distressed." She opened her eyes and looked at me. "She is very fond of you. She wouldn't. She is so sorry. She thinks you think." I say absolutely nothing to help her and I feel colder and colder. I can scarcely keep myself from sneering. "She's so sensitive," said Miss Wyman. "Rosa is very sensitive." My room-mate couldn't stand it. I didn't have any feelings at all. I felt bored.

"Miss Wyman," said my room-mate, "go ask her why she did it then. Tattling. Trying to get a drag, I suppose."

Miss Wyman looked terribly hurt but still pretty healthy.

"Rosa has a very strict sense of duty. She is a very honorable girl. She feels very badly." Miss Wyman hesitated and then said suddenly, "It's terrible to see her cry." None of us said anything.

"Good-night."

Victorine was standing in the closet door by now. Miss Wyman looked around at all of us, timid and hesitant. "Good-night."

"Good-night."

"Cripes," said Victorine, staring at me. "You've started something. The whole damn school is crying over you. Miss James."

"Miss James?"

"Yes, Mary Susan told me: Georgiana ought to be ashamed of herself. Miss James is in tears."

"Oh, my God," said my room-mate, delighted, "It must be even terribler to see Miss James cry than Rosa. Even terribler."

Victorine came and sat on the bed. I drew up my knees and the bed sagged and was uncomfortable. Victorine's flat grey eyes studied me. She seemed inattentive. "Long legs," she said, "Skinny."

*Chapter Eighteen*

NO STERN LETTER from grandpère; only the usual letter in his fine beautiful careful writing with a list of the misspelled words in my last letter to him. The "Grandpère" signed a little on the slant apart from the rest of the letter as if he felt separately a grandpa that had little to do with the chiseled words above. And I went to the school farm for a week end so I guess all is forgiven till the next time. I am exhausted from the farm week-end and sudden warm weather kills me. I can scarcely hold up my head and I haven't opened a book in days. Gym teacher and Miss McCormick chaperoned. There were eight of us. All of us slept in the same room, all the partitions having been removed upstairs in the little farmhouse, in white cots in a row. I didn't sleep at all with the giggling and

jumping about and feathers flying and Miss McCormick intermittently appearing and looking harassed. Also the gym teacher
who thinks she has a way with the girls. She pretends to be one
of us and gets terrible things said to her but she is dumb. She tries
to get invited to the girls' homes week ends but never does, and
works awfully hard to be asked as a chaperone when one of the
girls goes to the theatre or tea with a boy. She always wears a
middy blouse and short skirt and silk stockings and black
sneakers. She holds her legs quite wide apart and looks as though
she was going to swing dumbbells all the time. In gym class she
braids her hair in two braids and she practically hasn't got any.
The braids flip up and down as she jumps about and she sings
out, "One, two, three, one, two, three." She does the split and
things. Her legs are short and ugly. She has a lot of white teeth,
however, that she talks about, and admires in the mirror; bending over the bureau to it close, and drawing back her lips to
admire them. The poor thing is pretty ugly and so I suppose she
can't be blamed for carrying on the way she did. We heard a
scream from the back porch and then another, and "Oh, oh, oh."
I got there first. Gym teacher was bending over as though to
get out of her own way or as if things were spilling out of her
mouth and they were. She held both hands over her mouth to
keep what teeth remained inside and she kept on saying, "Oh,
oh, oh," and words we couldn't understand like somebody talking with her mouth full. Blood began to run down the corners
of her mouth and tears over her knuckles and fingers. She began
to stamp with her feet in anger and we got the words, "My beau-
ti-ful teeeeth."

"What happened. What happened?"

She cried harder, regular boo-hoo crying like a child, and
gingerly took one hand away from her mouth. She looked awful.
A couple of jagged ends remained of her two big front teeth.
In her hand she saw pieces of teeth and blood from a rapidly
swelling lip.

"Oh, oh, oh, my wonderful teeth," she wailed. She seemed

horrified at the queer lisping she was doing. She began to scream and cry. We all stood around; no one seemed to be able to feel sorry.

"How did it happen?"

She stamped her foot in her silent sneakers and pointed to the pump handle. "What dif-frence — when I'm spoiled for-ever."

We all began to feel that this thing was being overdone. But Brooks went up to her and put her soft arm around her. "Aw," she said, "Aw." Gym teacher jerked away. Brooks looked non-plused.

"The dentist," I said coldly, "will fix um."

"Yes," said everyone, "The dentist."

We finally got her upstairs and washed. Brooks did it. I went away. She was hanging on to her pieces of teeth and sobbing monotonously.

"How awful," said my room-mate later, "to have nothing but your teeth and then bust um." She stood on tiptoe and stared at her shimmering face in a cheap little mirror. "Am I pretty?" she said.

"You're terribly pretty," I said, "only your hair isn't any particular color at all." I remembered a disgusting simile Rosamond had made about my room-mate's lusterless coiled hair and didn't repeat it. She has light blue eyes wide apart and wood-brown lashes and arching brows. She always wets her finger and smooths them up and over after powdering her face. She has a small bright mouth and if there is a mirror around when she is talking to you, her attention wanders from her words to her face and she brings a dimple in and out in her cheek and begins to be vague in her speech. I wish she wouldn't do it. Rosamond and some others think she is awfully conceited.

"I'm going to undress," she said.

"Go on."

It didn't take long. Under her farm clothes, overalls and a shirt, she wore a fragile delicious pink chemise; short, half to the knee; no brassiere or panties at all. She pulled it off over her head and stood straight and lovely against the crude wide boarding of the room. Little high windows, curtains fluttering, let in a gentle light to her knees. She looked as if she were a torso on a pedestal. Slim and small, not skinny and tall like me. But not as pliable as me. Straight little shoulders; small flat breasts which she covers easily with each hand. Looking down she pushes back her elbows and fills her lungs with air.

"I've no more than a boy," she says doubtfully. And she hasn't. Her breasts are slightly squarish, hard and flat in this position but the center of each is as pink as a carnation.

"I don't care," she remarks relaxing and recovering a slight feminine curve, "I'll have a wet nurse."

"What," I say, absently, because I am quite lost in admiration of this small flat curving puppet. She is beginning to shiver. "For my kids," she said.

"Oh." I am not a bit interested in this remote possibility for any of us. Marriage, too, I put out of my mind glibly like death. My room-mate began turning and running about to keep herself warm. Her spine is invisible except where it dips in abruptly at the end; a little flat space no bigger than one's thumb. Her buttocks don't stick out foolishly like other people's but seem to push her pelvis forward flattening her small white stomach. They are easy and quiet when she walks and haven't that shift and change that other women's have even in their clothes. I've never liked it. I try to walk in front of people. Her thighs are flat on the sides and shaped like the top and middle of a *fleur de lys*. Her knees are small and tight and her calves show gently the double muscle that makes them higher on one side than the other; curving low between her legs from the front to the ankle and quite high and straight on the outside to the ankle. Her feet are pink; her toes are too short and curl under, not classic enough for me. There is a small white blister on one heel.

"Wow, gosh," Brooks lets out as she appears, out of breath, "what's zis? Shame." Her lower lip hangs down and her eyes are sticking out. My room-mate turns into a demon.

"Shame," she repeats at Brooks and sticks out her own lip. "Shame, Nasty," and begins to caper. She thumbs her nose and wiggles the extra fingers at Brooks; then she puts two forefingers to her head and bends her knees high. She tries to wag her tail and pretend she's a devil. Brooks holds on to herself with laughter; a bunch of girls appear and my room-mate gets suddenly shy. She jumps behind a square pillar and says, "Get out."

But they pull her out. She tries to resist them and curl up but they are unmerciful and stretch her out completely from one to the other. She looks crucified.

"You're hurting her," I say, "Go on, beat it. I hear Miss McCormick."

They let her go and skinny Louisa who has been looking on shakes her shoulders and purses her mouth and says, "It's disgusting."

"You're a fool," I said.

My room-mate doesn't seem to mind what's happened and curls up on the bed with a blanket.

Then everything began. The telephone in a cupboard downstairs began to ring and shake. No one is allowed calls at the farm. My room-mate sat up with her head on one side and put her finger to her lips.

"If that's Thompson. If he dared. I dared him."

She lay down quickly as Miss McCormick called upstairs, "Lucia!"

"I'm coming." She limped into her overalls and with a bare back dashed out holding up her toes to avoid splinters. She was up again in two minutes; so excited that she was quite calm.

"It was Thompson. For heaven's sake, listen. You're coming too."

"Sure."

"But you are."

Well, we got away after supper. Miss McCormick was reading aloud with the lamp shining through her thin yellow hair. We ran like mad down the straight dirt road, terribly excited.

My room-mate and Victorine and me. We looked like three thin ghosts in dresses turned white in the dark. Soon we had to stop for breath and caught hands and tried to see each other in the dark. The farmhouse light looked stupid and domestic behind us and ahead we began to hear the motors going by; only a few. We reached the diagonal road and some yards back along the road a car was parked, its lights dim and its engine going.

"Thompson," called Lucia.

"Shut up. Is it you?"

There were three boys but we could only see Thompson; the little light on the dashboard shining under his chin. He is attractive. Lucia has his picture and I look and look at it and have even drawn a copy of it. I am awfully excited. Victorine is already in the rumble seat with someone, though all we can see is his white collar. It is Lucia's idea to light a match in each face as we are introduced. I stare over the match at Thompson who I can't see at all in this sudden small brilliance. `

"Sit next to me, you," he said to me, "if you don't mind the gears."

"I'll straddle um," I said.

"Now what," said Lucia.

"Sit on Frick's lap. You'll have to." Thompson already had the car in gear. I lifted up one leg to let him do it and the cold steel slid along the inside of my other leg a little.

"Let's go. You'll probably all be fired for this," said Thompson.

Lucia was having some trouble adjusting herself to Frick's knees and was making monosyllabic remarks and Frick was just laughing a little and saying, "Are you comfortable? Is that better? You don't weigh anything. Sit down. There. Like that. Is that good?"

Lucia spread out and let her head fall back on Frick's shoulder.

"Oh," she said, "Miss McCormick is going to kill us. Just kill us — kill us, kill us, kill us."

I saw Frick drop his head. She drew away from me turning her back a little and facing Frick. I saw them trying to get their legs comfortable. I didn't hear any more conversation from them.

"Don't go so fast, it's jiggly back here," called Victorine.

Thompson stepped on the accelerator, shoving it down to the floor and I looked up at him for the first time. He put his hand on my knee and gave it a pat. Then he left it there lightly as we went faster and faster. "I like to go fast," I said.

He bent his head, "What?"

"Fast," I said, "I love it — as fast you can — go."

I had my lips close to his ear. He dipped his head quickly and my open mouth touched his cheek. He stayed that way and I didn't take my lips away. His face was smooth and cold and my lips felt warm and snug. He slowed down, put his arm around my shoulders and turned his mouth to me. I drew away quickly. He took his arm away and laughed.

"So you like to go fast," he said, "O.K." and the car leapt into the air and settled down on the straight hard road to a good seventy. After a while I looked at him again and when he didn't turn his head, I kept on staring. I looked at his hair and the sides of his eyes, down along his nose and his chin. His mouth was shut tight and there was a little upward curve to it. His white collar fits close around his neck and he has a bow tie. I stare at his hands, too, on the wheel and even look down at his feet on the floor. I can only see the shine of his shoes. I look back at his profile and look and look; at his ear and his jaw. After a while we turn back. No one has thought of the time. The stars have come out and it is cold. My teeth are chattering.

"Look at my teeth, Thompson," I say.

I open my lips and show them jumping up and down. He takes my hand and holds it tight on my lap. I let my fingers crawl up his sleeve where it feels very nice. We stop and I have a little difficulty getting my fingers out from under his cuff. He laughs and waits till I finish. We all hop out on the ground that's a little spongy hard with late frost. I am shaking now uncontrollably with cold and excitement. Victorine's boy is standing holding both her hands and saying something to her. She is saying, "Yes. Yes, of course — of course I do. Yes, I will honest and truly. Yes."



"Beat it, you kids," says Thompson. "Come on. Let us know if you're fired."

He doesn't look at me as he drives off and Frick sings out, "So long."

"Tomorrow," screams Lucia after him. We start along home in silence. I start to jig and run, I am so cold. Ahead of us is the entire lot.

"Oh, Lord," says Lucia. "There they come."

"Shut up," says Victorine.

"Where have you been?"

"Oh walking."

"Well, Miss McCormick. Miss McCormick is just about. Miss McCormick is. She's got fits. Miss McCormick is absolutely sick. She's crying and everything. Where have you been? She's nuts."

"Oh Lord," said Lucia.

Victorine speaks up. "We haven't been anywhere; look. Do you see; nowhere. I'll run ahead.

"I'll come, too," I said.

"Miss McCormick," we called.

In one of the small downstairs rooms we found her; a couple of girls hanging over her helplessly. She was dabbing her eyes and sniffing. She didn't seem surprised, or even pleased to see us. She had gotten sort of used to our being gone, I guess, and was forgetting what she was crying about.

"We're sorry, Miss McCormick. Please don't cry. We were just walking," said Victorine. "We got so far," I said. "We didn't realize it was so late," said Victorine. "We got a little bit lost," I said. "Yes," said Victorine, "quite a lot lost." "We heard an owl," I said. "We ran home as fast as we could," said Victorine. "It's beautiful out," I said suddenly.

Miss McCormick looked up, quite red around the eyes.

"Oh, my dears, how could you."

"I know it's awful," said Victorine.

"I have been so worried. I am responsible for all of you. I thought, oh, I thought," said Miss McCormick. She leaned back her head and closed her eyes. With one hand she raised a little glass bottle of smelling salts to her nose, waved it gently back and forth and put out the other to us. Victorine took it and Miss McCormick raised it to her cheek.

"Thank God, you are safe."

Victorine didn't look a bit embarrassed. "Of course we're safe," she said.

"Yes," said Lucia.

"We're safe," I said.

Upstairs Victorine was in bed quickly. She raised her head on her elbow and said to Lucia on the next bed, "I'm crazy about him. I don't suppose I'll ever see him again."

"Good-night."

"Good-night!"

"Good-night."

Brooks, a slow poke, last to get to bed, stood in a slinky kimono, her hand on the light. She looked in our direction.

"Liars."

She pulled out the light so hard that the little chain jumped up and fell back several times.

## Chapter Nineteen

AND NOW SOME-
thing really terrible has happened. It is all in the papers. The
girls read it. Miss James made a speech after prayers last night.
Flower's brother Charles is dead. The paper said he jumped out
of the window. Miss James said that the headmaster said that he
was a somnambulist. He walked out of the window in his sleep.
At two o'clock. His room-mate didn't know until morning. Miss
James says we must all try and help Flower because she is coming over here to stay. Her stepmother has a trained nurse and Dr.
Seymour is away. Miss James said Charles was a dear little fellow.
Flower adored him. "She will need all our sympathy and help.
Girls, I hope you will be thoughtful and kind." Her chin
trembled. I looked at Mam'selle who wasn't paying attention.

Fräulein looked stern as though one of us had done it. Miss Haynes was studying her prayer book. To all our horror, Janie began to giggle. Rosa looked terribly cross-eyed at her; her big flat shoes sticking out hard in front of her and Vera stood very still with tears running down her cheeks.

"There will be no dancing tonight."

I looked at Fredericka and she made a face at me. After prayers Frieda came up to me and pulled at my arm.

"I've got the paper in my room," she said, "Come on."

"No," I said, "I don't want to." I remembered our all staring at Charles' picture in Flower's room and Flower breaking the china bowl. Miss James, instead of disappearing as usual, stood around, her big black eyes taking us all in. All of us looked at the door at the same time. Flower. She had on a black dress, her cheeks were pink and her eyes wide open, and no sign of tears. She had a box of chocolates and began passing them around.

"This kind has got nuts in them," she said. "I've got a new wrist watch," she said. She began to laugh and said, "Aren't we dancing tonight?"

"Flower!"

"Yes, Miss James."

"You had better go to your room."

Flower hesitated.

"Now!"

Flower looked stubborn and some of the color left her cheeks. "Why?"

Miss James became gentle. "I think you had better go to your room and think things over by yourself. You can't realize."

Flower shut her teeth together hard and then opened her mouth and said coldly,

"You mean Charles? Charles jumped. Charles jumped out of the window. He jumped out of the window and killed himself." Then she said, "What of it?"

Mam'selle looked up. She walked over to Flower and took her arm.

"*Fleur*, we will talk. Somewhere. No?"

Flower looked pleased and shy, "Yes, Mam'selle."

"Flower," said Miss James, "you will come to my study in one hour."

"Yes, Miss James."

My room-mate said to me afterwards, "She'll make her realize all right."

But Flower passed a group of us in the hall when she came out of Miss James's study and said, "He didn't fall. He jumped."

Tonight Victorine appeared in our room as usual after lights. She sat on the window sill in boy's pajamas that hiked up her calves when she sat down. Her legs are cream color and she's got on beaded moccasins with black fur around the top. I heard her say to my room-mate, "He felt me all over."

She got up and shook herself to get the legs of her pants down. A good six inches of slim leg still shows. I can see her because the room is lit from the street. She comes over, bends down and gives me a kiss on the ear.

"Good-night, beautiful."

Her short hair brushed my cheek and it began to itch. The bed squeaked.

"Get out," I said, "Here comes Fräulein."

Victorine streaked quickly for the closet door, got halfway through and crashed over my hat box.

"Cripes," I heard her say in a loud voice. At once there was a knock. I shut my eyes hard. Neither of us answered. Another knock and the door simultaneously opened. I can feel my eyelids shaking but I relax my face and appear to sleep. Fräulein tiptoes in and peers at my room-mate. I look beneath my lids. My room-mate is lying on her stomach, her face hid in the pillows. She is as still as death. Fräulein turns gently, lifts her feet like a cat, humps over and cautiously makes her way out. She has a screwed-up, almost gentle look on her face. "The old fool," whispers my room-mate. We both wiggle around a little and soon are dead asleep.

# Chapter Twenty

*J*EAN HAS BEEN
giving me a lecture; her foolish little heart-shaped face serious
and superior; turning to my sister and asking, "Isn't it true?"

"What?" I say.

"I went because they asked and asked me," I said. "I went
with Nancy B. It was boring."

"Nancy B. is foolish in the head," said Jean, "and Spencer
oughtn't to be allowed. Miss James ought to. Really. Isn't it so,
Caroline?"

"What's the matter with Spencer?" I said. "She's nice. I like
her."

Spencer is recently about again a lot; hardly seen for weeks;
and stalks unsmiling up and down the aisles. Sometimes she

hesitates at my desk and I smile at her. There is an imperceptible movement of her straight mouth. She runs her knuckles along my desk and I watch without moving. It's as if a ghost passed by. I even get the impression that no one has seen her but me. Once in the hall upstairs it was the same. She was coming down. I stood and waited to let her come. She gave me that same smile, that is no smile. I spoke but I don't think she answered. She went across to the top of the next flight and down. I saw her brown head disappear. Tears came to my eyes and I said to myself, "What is it?"

"Have you ever looked at her sister?" said Jean, pink in the face, "Have you ever?"

"Yes. No."

Unlike Spencer, this girl wears a constant grin, teeth apart. I don't know her name. I've never heard it called. She is as ugly as the devil. Black coarse hair, uncombed; black eyes, bright and senseless. Pale sick face and funny teeth. There is a heavy growth of stubby hair along her upper lip. I've never seen any-one, teacher or girl, speak to her. I can remember her going out the side door from study hall, an armful of books, grinning good-bye to all of us; to our backs. After the first shock of seeing her, we are absolutely unaware of her. And when Jean brings her up now, it seems as though it were long ago that I had seen her while really she never misses a day at school.

"She looks like something vile," said Jean.

"She looks like a dog," I said. "I don't mean like a dog really but like a girl that looks like a dog."

"She's filthy looking," said Jean.

"Jean," I said, "Do you see what I mean — not like a dog. But like a person like a dog."

"The thing is," said Jean, "there's something awful about that family."

"People don't look like that without," said my sister.

"People who have children that look like that have got some-thing awful," said Jean.

"Spencer gave me her picture in basketball costume," I said.

"You can't be friends with her," said my sister.

"Go get it," said Jean.

I ran along the hall into our room and scrambled around in my bureau drawer.

"What you looking for," said my room-mate.

"Spencer's picture."

"She's homely."

"She's got something awful in her family," I said. "Jean's bawling me out. I have to go."

I showed it to Jean. Our three heads bent over it. Spencer looking straight at us unsmiling. In middy and short bloomers, her long black stockings wrinkling over the knees.

"My word," exclaimed Jean. " 'From a man who loves you.' "

She stepped back and squinted at me.

"Disgusting," said Caroline.

"What does she mean," said Jean. "Did she kiss you?"

"Spencer!" I said. "Kiss me!"

I began looking at the inscription myself. "It's because she's dressed like that," I said. "Spencer is nice."

"She doesn't even speak to me," I went on.

Jean began to look bored. "Well, anyway," she said.

"Imagine getting her picture taken in bloomers," said Caroline. She began to brush her long yellow hair and the effort made her face pink. Jean watched her. Caroline brushed it, dipping her head and letting it fall in long slow ripples.

"Oh," she said, letting her arm fall and lifting her head. "What a nuisance, my hair is so long." Jean looked at my sister's radiant beauty and grew cold with anger.

"Why don't you cut it off," she snapped. "I have to cut mine off. I couldn't stand all that hair. I cut mine off all the time. Eight inches I cut off last time."

Caroline recommenced brushing with an aristocratic look on her face. I didn't dare laugh out; it was funny to think of Jean's soft pink clinging hair ever getting further down than her neck. It creeps and crawls like new ivy.

# Chapter Twenty-one

CAROLINE WOKE
me at quarter of seven. I was frightened and sat up quickly. I had
dreamt in the night that I had let my arm hang over the side of
the bed and a dog had snapped off my fingers. I looked at them.

"What," I said.

Caroline went on shaking me.

"Aunt is very ill. We have to take the eight o'clock train.
Miss James. Get up. Put on your blue serge dress." My room-
mate woke up.

"What the hell," she said.

By this time I had on my stockings and had to take them off.

"Lend me a pair of stockings," I said, wringing my hands.

"Aunt. I have to take the eight o'clock train. Oh dear." I began to cry and it made my eyes sting. My room-mate handed me a cold wet washcloth.

"Come on, stop it," she said. "She'll be all right. Come on. Stop it. Never mind."

She washed my face for me. We got to the train in the school station wagon and Caroline bought the tickets with money Miss James had given us. There hadn't been an extra teacher to send with us. "I guess you'll be all right together," said Miss James. "Don't speak to anyone."

"Of course," said Caroline with dignity.

I don't remember the trip home. I remember that only Page met us as we stepped off the train.

"How is Aunt?" we both said.

He took both our little bags in one hand. We stared in his face.

"It's not your Aunt, it's Mrs. Lord," he said. He looked frightened and helpless. He got us in the front seat where we liked to sit and stepped in himself slamming the door and hanging his head.

"Grandmère," I said.

"Grandmère," said Caroline.

"How sick, how, Page?" I said, "Oh please."

I was terrified. I knew the answer. I shut my eyes and the tears slipped down my face. I didn't make any noise.

"Be brave," said Page. His lower lip was shaking and the tears stood out on his long fringe of lashes. Caroline was very white the way she was when she sprained her ankle.

Grandpère stood, grey and shaking, in his study door as we came in. I kissed him and stood back. I wasn't crying any more and his lost appearance was terrible. I couldn't speak to him. He looked very small. He turned and went back into his study. Aunt got us some tea and bread and butter.

"I can't," I said.

Caroline looked angry and haughty. She went off to her room. Aunt's large green eyes filled with tears.

*153*

"It was just as she would have wished," she said. "She was not sick a day."



I turned away.

"She was standing at her mirror. I heard her fall."

I didn't say anything. I began to feel like a stranger.

"Your grandpère knelt beside her. She only said, 'Jasper.'"

I feel cold and angry; then I feel nothing; simply nothing. It's as if nothing had happened. I pick up my hat and walk upstairs. I go past, on the landing, one of the portraits; my great-great-aunt. It's been varnished and is slippery in the half light. "They've ruined it, varnishing it," I said to myself. At the top of the stairs I turn naturally toward my grandmother's room. The door is shut.

"Oh the door is shut," I say and go down the hall to my own room and look at myself in the mirror. I turn and look out the window, the sun is going down. I feel it on my face. There is a delivery wagon at the back door. The boy is easing out a large basket with brown bags full of things and a loaf of bread and a couple of cans with green labels. Grandpère won't eat canned things. He is going to say to grandmère, "What have we a garden for," and grandmère will say, "I thought for a change." There isn't anything in the garden now, I think. I look across at it. The tops of little frame houses reflect the sun. Henry is solemnly pushing a wheelbarrow. I turn back to the mirror. My own eyes say nothing to me. "What is the matter," I say out loud. "What is the matter," I add impatiently.

Chapter Twenty-two

WE CAME BACK TO
school in black dresses. Caroline looks very pretty in hers but is
solemn and distant. I feel conspicuous and ashamed in mine. I
feel dark and sullen and unhappy in it. It is high at the neck and
scratchy. It is too long and my legs look like sticks. My wrists
look brown and helpless. My hat is stiff black straw and hurts
my forehead. I don't take it off the whole trip and my head aches.
The conductor looks from one to the other as he punches our
tickets. A middle-aged woman turns her Pullman chair half
around and stares at us. She says something to the conductor
about us and he shrugs his shoulders. A man across the aisle who
has a brief case and is making accounts with an unlit cigar in

his mouth, looks at Caroline's ankles and then her face. She takes out a little red book and starts reading. She is frowning. It is Machiavelli's *Prince*.

Back at school Caroline runs upstairs and Miss Haynes comes to me in the hall. She has her chin raised and is trying to see me through the bottom of her glasses. She puts her hand on my arm and says,

"The girls have missed you."

I don't reply and she pats my arm.

"There," she says.

The study-hall door bursts open and several girls dash out like traveling hounds let out of a freight car. They see me and stop; then walk by me without looking at me. Up the stairs they are off again. Fredericka bounces out, sees me, and says,

"Hello! When did you get back. Did you have a good time?"

"Yes, thank you," I say miserably.

"Darling," says Fredericka blushing red, "I'm sorry."

"It's all right," I say.

"I'll take your bag up," she says, and precedes me up the stairs. My room-mate comes running and hugs me. My hat comes off and rolls in a circle. Someone picks it up and looks at it curiously. Flower is standing staring at my black dress.

"How long have you got to wear that," she says.

*     *     *     *     *

And so this long quotation has taken your mind off the girl I am writing about. In her journal she has told you nothing of herself; something about others. She simply seems to have been there. No one saw anything odd in a girl who seemed to be having fun and was; but it was a kind of neuter fun, an excitement of almost a literary kind; a respite, too, from certain rules and regulations of grandpère's, but the respite was only apparent. Please note that she did not enter into the passionate bisexual adolescent love life of her companions. That love life that seems to be mostly confusion, a compelling sporadic interest in both sexes and all ages: little boys, old men, schoolteachers, contemporaries; as if the body hadn't decided yet what it was going to be: male or female; whether it was young or old; mythologically uncertain, Hermaphroditic. This strange love life keeps the adolescent continuously attached to this and that, incontinent; an absurd polygamy, unable to concentrate on the Great Books but concentrating on something, learning to pay attention, perhaps. It is not important. Neither was Georgiana's slightly off-side growing-up important. It is true she walked straight through it thinking of something else, a little scared by the confusion around her but not very, a little curious about what was going on but not enough to ask questions. She kept her head. Only her walking straight through it as if she were taking the 7:45 in the Grand Central Station was characteristic and besides, her successful, if unconscious, avoidance of sex. Grandpère had been an excellent tutor and the big red bull she forgot. Affection, that minor poem on passion, you will remember she had taught herself to suppress as a kind of resistance against people whom she did not care to have witness any weakness of hers. And so she comes into port with a little flag flying, "Owner Aboard." When she steps ashore, however, things begin to happen; and she will find a lover in every port. The interim of her adolescence is over; not so difficult for her as for most because she didn't notice it; and now, in her maturity, she will return to her childhood. It will be a continued story, as it were. She will behave in her grown-up life as she was surely conditioned to behave in her childhood, and if there were such an idiom as *raison de faire* that is what I would have called this fatalistic story of Georgiana.

*Part Three*

Part Three

THE STORY OF
a woman must of necessity and by definition be a love story: a
woman knows what comes first and keeps it ahead of her; she
never confuses occupational therapy with primary causes; she
doesn't mix her metaphors; she prefers happiness to content-
ment; at least the woman of whom I speak is this special clarifica-
tion of sex of which I wish to speak; she is this femininity, this
little woman who in spite of talents, logic and brains sticks to her
last; does what she does best, makes the most of her personal and
feminine nature: loves. And if it appears that she wastes her
talents, her brains, her consciousness, it is only because these
things are secondary, peripheral, a kind of rose-colored back-

drop to her sweet existence in the arms of her lovers. And oddly enough, I mean by her lovers the people she loved; the others meant nothing to her, she had absolutely no interest in them, other than a kind of transitory pity born of her own sufferings which, powerful as they were, left little room for handholding with intransitives. She only loved the ones she loved. I shall therefore skip that quite long line of everlasting lovers who finally married someone else, who sporadically wrote her, telephoned her, used the means of communication at their elbows, kept her picture in an old watch; who remembered her at odd times when they were ill, sad, unhappy, about to be divorced, married, die; who in spite of circumstance, reality, education, thought of her gently, believed in her, loved her, but of whom she was unaware because she did not love them; who gave her no comfort, no security, any more than a parent who lives in the next room when one's heart-interest is in Paris.

There is no doubt that the girl was polygamous, polygamous in the sense that everyone who loves steadfastly is polygamous: the constant everlasting search for one's first love whom one cannot remember gives one the character of a Knight seeking the Grail; the ruthlessness, passionate insistence, integrity, the heartlessness of one who knows he is right characterized this girl whose wordly behavior appeared to be unconventional, even unscrupulous to the ordinary person, the moderate citizen whose hopes are measurable, whose wandering eye despises the objects it seeks, whose ten-percent tips bring light to no one's brow.

She devoted her life after adolescence to love! I say after adolescence because during that time and before it she was unaware of her future, her career. She was frightened, superstitious, almost bisexual in her intermittent desire for power and love of weakness: frail sweet surrender, fear; and that intermediate state described as the maternal instinct during which she put doll clothes on a puppy only to end in mild and timid torture of him, taking him back to her heart, her small breast, letting him sneak up between her legs; and then, after kissing her cousins, hating them, was filled with remorse as if she had harmed them, like any husband who has mistakenly married the woman he merely desires. All these things prepared, but did not protect, this girl. It was as if she had studied, or been taught at least, reading, writing and arithmetic thoroughly and persistently only to find when she was given a book to read, a problem to solve, a letter to translate, that her education was not applicable. Her childhood loves were merely analogous, then, to the loves of her maturity and as an analogy is a parallelism and as two straight lines can never meet, except themselves, I understand, so our heroine gained nothing from her early childhood experience, nothing, I mean, in a practical sense which helped her to solve her later love problems. She did not, however, lose sight of that perfumed horizon parallel to which she traveled and which she dreamily recognized as her early love life.

That her education in love, therefore, was informal is an understatement and at thirteen it was over; her school days serving as a respite between the things that had happened to her and the things she would do. The daydreaming girl became a woman of action which is not a paradox at all; her actions, however, were singular, unique, based on the continued story of her personal intention and consequently seemed odd, queer, arrogant, without sequence, only to those who were not the confidantes of her rationality, not the puppets of her perfectly sensible theatre and these others were practically everybody. "Poor child," one might say, and then almost immediately contradict oneself, "Happy idiot." No name calling or encyclopedia, however, can give the x or y, or answer Q.E.D. to the behavior of a steadfast girl whose lovers outnumbered her years and whose experience in love taught her absolutely nothing. In this way and this alone she resembles the rest of us with the exception that the rest of us lose time, get off to a bad start, by treating the new love as if he were the last one. This arithmetical carrying-over of small numbers puzzles the lover on whom it is practiced even when he is unconsciously doing the same thing himself to his new darling.

She found, bright girl, that experience in men was experience in the last one but never the next one. That what one learns about a man one learns about him alone; scrap, therefore, what you know about John when you begin with Edward; just as an artist is no longer able to "see," when he mistakenly thinks that because he has drawn a hand before he can draw it again, who thinks that a face is a memory of face, that it is two eyes, a mouth, and a nose, as a child symbolically does; so, she learned that a woman makes a mistake when she treats a man as if he were the last one. (And, besides, the fun of variation is lost to her.) In other words Georgiana learned to treat life as if it were a series of rooms and as she entered and left each she closed doors behind her, not like Nora (this time), with a slam, but gently, gratefully, sometimes absent-mindedly, already anticipating the next chamber. She did find, however, to continue the metaphor, that the light switch was nearly always in the same place to her left as she entered and all she had to do was put out her hand to flood the room with light. I do not mean that Georgiana was as completely able as all this, however, to ignore her experience and her errors, mistakes; in details, on the contrary, she was not always intelligent and in fearfulness like any other lover she often missed her cue, trumped an ace, discarded from weakness rather than strength. But sometimes in succession or at the same time she staggered her lovers and what she learned from one in her reticence she taught the other one who resisted her in his, which is rather different and fairly intelligent. This was particularly true of the two *affaires* that for lack of space I shall confine myself to relating as best I can, missing much, I am afraid, that might give you a different opinion of Georgiana; but someone else may have that other story which it is always possible to tell of a woman according to the ability of the author and the bulk of the woman's behavior to choose from.

Georgiana was as fresh when she took on the love affair before the last (in my list) as when she passionately loved the first dark man in her life, whom she allowed to kiss her without hesitation (this is it!) and from whom she asked nothing but just that: kissing. She never forgot the charm of that first warm kiss (Mr. Bullard didn't count, remember?) which did not embarrass or frighten her and their two eager faces submerged in a kind of scissor-like mutual benefaction, in an untiring repetition, which in his absence she repeated in her imagination until it is a wonder she did not die of exhaustion from that one long kiss. It was the prototype upon which all her first kisses must be founded no matter how skilled the lover in kissing, adept, original, later on in his love; the moment when she knew her lover was about to kiss her and she him, at just the right split second when there was no drawing back, no hesitation, no interruption, became the most delightful conscious moment in love-making to her and the change of characters seemed to have nothing to do with the quality of the kiss. I would not like to say that it was for this moment that she sometimes appeared to hurry through her lovers, pick quarrels with them, let them break her heart, but there is no doubt that each first kiss was as good as the last; there was at its culmination no room for regret. I am glad that I can really believe and say this at the risk of making my readers think that here was a flippant girl, a callous flirt, because Georgiana had a capacity for pain, poor thing, physical and psychic; she was more sorrowful than gay, deadly in earnest, and if she was happy in her first kiss she was not so in love: to her the thing was serious and only one man made her laugh during love-making and he her last love (in this story), the one I shall tell about, that blue-eyed lover for whom she had no psychic regard and from whom she learned much that enabled her to understand her past love life, and likewise to fear the future no-longer-innocent wanderings of her libido which had not known such love was likely.

Georgiana, then, was always in love. Her scenic life, the things that happened around her she did not notice. She traveled light, let us say, and kept her head, although the reader may believe that this is true scarcely within the metaphor as he reads on, carrying only the strict necessities and the changing light and tone of her feelings. I do not want to picture her as a traveler, a little girl with a suitcase and one-night stands, however, because it is not true, really: love came to her, and surprisingly often, and all she can be said to have done was look up and smile; but even this is metaphorical. It is true that love to her was like a dance, a ball; she had plenty of partners but even as she danced seemingly happily with one at a time, she saw someone across the room that she wanted, whose head was turned away; the one who did not dance. Neither was she surprised to find him as skillful as the rest and she finally not quite at ease in his arms, and across the room again a man who did not dance who reminded her of someone else. Love gave her life a direction, a meaning, and only her partners changed. To other people and in her daily life she appeared forgetful; unobserving; lacking in beliefs; enthusiasms; offhand about politics, rules and regulations; careless even callous; unaware of current events, Our Town; bored with history; unable to add up a bridge score; a little superior; going some place but where? looking for something but what? bemused; but in reality, within her own scheme, her orbit, her love life, never off the beam for a second. She carried in her head a surprisingly detailed and daily mounting set of sweet facts and fancies, integrated, neat, brilliantly arranged and cared for, and she walked lightly, on tiptoe, among her dear possessions. People in airplanes, streetcars and in church stared at that face whose shining gaze did not stop at theirs but looked out and beyond so intently, until, perhaps, it would not be an exaggeration to say that obeying the law in relativity that there is no such thing as a straight line these dark eyes were seeing happily into themselves from the back, having come a long way, too. This search that was not a search but a kind of active passivity kept her so preoccupied that she was unaware of the passage of time or the fact that she was loved by others than the ones she loved in succession, and she missed, I think I can say, the loving care and protection that was actually lavished upon her by these others who failed to see that like a bucket of water she was safe as long as she was in action and in no need of their apprehensive care: they need not have feared for her.

At the risk of seeming to wish to finish the story of her last love before it is begun I would like to make it clear now while it is at least temporarily so to me that in seeking love she found a person and finding the person she lost love. I have said that she appeared to prefer loving to being loved, unconscious even as she seemed throughout of this last fact, but the resistance which necessarily occurred in the beloved object's behavior taught her at the same time a desire for comfort and reassurance, unused as her sex was of being the subject rather than the object of love. Then it was that she appreciated when it came the love of Michael, that one, which, given the opportunity, sought her out, enlivened her femininity, made her feel secure in her appeal, warm, sweet, gentle; it did her good; but it was temporary, to her not real, only a respite after which, at first, until she became entirely his own, she enjoyed without the handicap of doubt her unrequited love in the person of the one before the last of whom I shall speak. These two loves went hand in hand for awhile and like a sister between two brothers she turned from one to the other, asking not for integration, for everything in one but something in each. She got it.

It is true Michael had seen her first; she had been innocent of his first glance, but at his second, circumstances, at least her way of accepting them, had changed and she looked at him and saw him. It had been a week of close association with the dark-eyed, everlasting, unrequited one whom she loved dearly; a week of response, she felt, on her side alone and she was weary, depressed, even frightened, at what she felt was a tie she could not break although she was the lover, perhaps because she was. With a degree of horror, a cold spell in her heart and a real shiver her thoughts came together with the result: "Only a new love will free me;" and was sure no new love would come; positive. Fear returned; she could not get over it. This queer fear of the responsibility of love which she had no right to, being a woman, but which she had acquired, or seemed to acquire, no doubt, by taking the initiative with Eric made her uneasy and jumpy and that is why this one's first look had gone by; she had not known that here was the new love whom she did not expect, and without the panorama she was in she would not naturally have felt any quick response to this lad, her junior, and blue-eyed like any cousin, spoiled, too, as one could see by his stance, his impudence, his treatment of her in conversation as if he were sure she was his superior but he would not be intimidated, and a kind of childish arrogance, lack of pity, but sickening wish for affection; a motherless boy. At the second look things began to happen. "What, again, it's not possible," each one said and looked away. Repeating the look and for a little longer, each one said, "Is it possible?" Invisibly each shook his head, "No, I won't." and looked again. Here a split in identicalness of thought took place:

He: Perhaps.
She: It can't be true.
He: This time I may fail.
She: He is beautiful.
He: It would be my luck.
She: He is a sweet love, he is a darling.
He: Just when I really mean it.
She: He is good.
He: This is it.
She: He is good and I am good.
He: I'll lose her.
She: How wonderful.
He: I can't stand it. I hate it.
She: I want to go home and remember him.
He: She wears a ring. She is married.
She: Friendship.
He: That won't matter.
She: A darling friend.
He: But this one is good.

She: I mean it.
He: I'll take it easy.
She: I feel pink all over, I am pretty.
He: It can't be helped.
She: I am happy now.
He: This is forever — that's the difference.
She: It can't last.
He: I'll make love to her very slowly.
She: Oh, how awful that it can't last.
He: So she won't be frightened.
She: I'll make a mistake, I am sure to.
He: I am not kidding myself, she is as good as gold.
She: He will make me unhappy.
He: Just when I want her so, I can't have her.
She: I'll try not to show my unhappiness.
He: I'll try.
She: I want to look into his eyes not at them.
He: I feel that I know how to do it.
She: I am doing it.
He: But do what?
She: I am doing it some more.
He: I love her.
She: Here I go — deeply — deeply.
He: I love her.
She: Deep into the depths of deepness.
He: She is looking into my eyes not at them.
She: I feel as if I were going down a long stairway.
He: I am frightened.
She: I am all alone but I am safe.
He: I am lost.
She: I am excited and sure of myself.
He: Don't.
She: I am bathing in a pool.
He: Must I submit?
She: I love him.

He: I love her.

She: I love him.

He: I love her. (I swear to God I do.)

She: How wonderful it is to be free again.

He: I am a fool when I was free to entangle myself.

And so their first conversation was a silent one.

Their second, out loud, follows:

She: How do you do; hello.

He: Thanks for letting me come.

She: You should be pleased. I don't like people much.

He: I am. Why did you let me?

She: I thought.

He: Just another admirer?

She: How horrid.

He: I apologize.

She: I don't like you.

He: I'm not likable.

She: I'm sorry I let you come.

He: You ought to read Marx.

She: Ought should only be used in the first person singular.

He: You're used to being treated as a brain . . . .

She: I'm not used to anything.

He: You're a woman to me.

She: All right. Stop it.

He: I don't want the usual love affair.

She: Nobody suggested it.

He: The same thing, the same thing, with that everlasting common denominator. You can't talk to a woman when you're making love to her. There's no conversation. Everything stops when it begins. It's the end of everything.

She: What are you complaining about?

He: I don't want it.

She: Oh, shut up.

He: You're the most beautiful woman I have ever seen. You are lovely.

She: (Nothing.)

He: You believe in things; you care about things; your emotion is deep and your every gesture is beautiful and meaningful; nothing is wasted; your movements are filled with feeling; what a machine, how desirable.

She: How nice you talk.

He: Will you have lunch with me?

She: I'd love to.

At lunch:

He: I'm hungry, I want a big lunch.

She: I don't think I do.

He: Let's have all this. Why did you come?

She: I wanted to. I'll make you a good salad.

He: It's not enough. Do you always do what you want to?

She: No. — With a little garlic around the bowl; it has to be a wooden bowl. Waiter, I want a wooden bowl, if you have it, please, a plain wooden chopping bowl, no shellac, and salt and pepper; just plain lettuce, no, none of that stuff, it tickles, just plain lettuce, not iceberg lettuce either. (*To him*) Isn't iceberg lettuce awful? Lettuce, it must be very dry or you will have to send a towel; I mean it. (*To him*) Do you want tomato ketchup and hot things in it or just a plain French dressing? All right. Waiter, a big spoon, a little sugar. No, I *don't* want to make the dressing in another dish. I want a big spoon, a big one; I make the dressing in the spoon; bring me a fork. (*To him*) My grandfather taught me. And, Waiter, then I'll have a lamb chop, double, and pink, please, all the way through, maybe a little piece of fresh mint with it but never mind if you haven't it. Mr.——— will have the table d'hote. I'll take everything at once, please. I like it all at once.

He: You know what you want, don't you?

She: May I have a cocktail?

He: I'll buy a bottle of wine.

She: Oh, no, that is too expensive because you don't want Californian, do you? It's ghastly, and I don't know why it should be; they've got the same grapes, everything. They've got everything but they won't take time. There's plenty of time but they won't take it. Loving care is what is needed, just plain loving care, don't you think? May I have my Martini very dry — you will have to say *very* dry, tell them four to one or it will taste vermouthy, and a little piece of lemon peel.

He: I like to do things myself.

She: Do, then. Talk to me again. I love it.

He: I don't feel like it.

She: But am I just to wait?

He: I don't want to be told.

She: I'm waiting.

He: (Nothing.)

She: (tries something else) I couldn't read Marx. He is stupid.

He: You don't appreciate him. You're a Platonist, anyone can see.

She: I know it. It's easier to understand abstract things than Marx's practical talk and stuff.

He: Have you read, "The Dialectics of History"?

She: How can you use the word dialectic when talking about Marx. Oh, I see, it's used the way Tolstoy uses it when he said about the Napoleonic Wars: "War is a movement of peoples, from East to West..."

He (irritated): No, that's not it.

She (annoyed): Of course it is — dialectic is a way not a thing. People say dialectics — that's bad you know — it isn't right at all; it's not a noun.

He (looks and looks): I like you. I like you.

She (she is cautious): I like you too, part of the time, temporarily, as it were. I like you temporarily.

He: What! Holding hands! Isn't it wrong to hold hands?

She: No, no it isn't.

He: It is wrong. Holding hands with a married woman at lunch.

She: You think I think it is. How did you know? And why do you talk in capitals?

He: Do you? Think it is?

She (lying): No.

He: I am moral too, just as moral, very moral.

She: But who told you? I don't believe it. It is good to be friends.

He: That's what I want. Badly.

She: But friendship is based on love.

He: Yes?

She: Of course.

He: How?

She: First people must love each other; then after that perhaps they are friends but not very often.

He: Is love a word? It depends on who says it.

She: No, no, but people think friendship may be had for the asking. It's hard work, and love, love is the foundation.

He: And easy?

She: No, no, but love is the foundation.

He: I want to build the foundation. Let us do it. Right away. Waiter! Check please!

She: You are laughing.

May I interrupt these lovers to continue that they had luncheon every day and then they went home to her house, and here is one of their conversations there:

He: Here we are. I must go.

She: Have a little glass of brandy and run along.

He: I love you, I don't know why, I love you. Here, here in my arms, I feel your body; I know it; I want it. Oh, sleep . . . sleep . . . I want to sleep with you. Not just that — but sleep; all it means; all it implies; less than it means and more; oh, Woman, Woman.

She: (Nothing.)

He: Here is my mouth; here is yours; look. Do you mind little noises; excuse the funny noises, please.

She: Darling; darling; baby.

He: What?

She: Baby.

He: I can't hear you.

She: Nothing, little heart.

He: I cannot stand it; what shall I do?

She: What is wrong; don't cry.

He: I am crying, that is what.

She: Don't cry, little thing.

He: There, I push you away.

She: Your mouth is red.

He: Yours is pale.

She: Do you love me?

He: No.

She: No?

He: More . . . more . . . more . . . .

She: Wait.

He: Now. I will; I will.

She: No . . . no . . . no . . . .

He: Don't think I won't. Here is your ear.

She: Go home, go home now, goodbye, oh my ear, how wonderful.

He: I won't come back.

She: Goodbye, darling, oh, my ear.

He: You are sending me away.

She: No, dear, no darling. I'm not.

He: You are sending me away.

She: I will kiss you once more. Here I am.

He: I really love you, love you.

She: And I, . . . you're hurting me; stop it.

He: What?

She: I love you, too.

He: Then let me stay.

She: Please, darling, please. No, no.

He: Goodbye.

She: Goodbye; tomorrow? Goodbye.

He: I don't know.

She: What time?

He: Who knows.
She: Goodbye, darling.
He: Goodbye.
She: Goodbye. Tomorrow.

"And That's the He and the She of it," one might say with Joyce. To continue: his approach, address, was as if he was at golf or he too at a dance: he placed a hand on her either hip and gently shoved her to one side then the other; she gave to this manipulation as if he were the wind, with only the resistance that a white sail gives in order to proceed and a sweet breeze indeed that lifted her spirit instead of her hair and fanned her emotions, neglected in her intellectual, unrequited love, as nice as you please. She stared at his mouth, or felt that she looked at his eyes with her mouth: his eyes and mouth seemed to change places and she did not know whether her eyes were on his mouth or her mouth was looking at his eyes. The line between his closed lips seemed to be duplicated in pain across her chest from the tip of one breast to the other and this mixed-up facial and bodily geography taught her the true, straight and passionate desire that amoeba-like does not take into account detail or design but is all wish, all verb, all being, and unshackled by this and that: one becomes all mouth, all eyes, all hands, or all legs like inter-winding fraternal columns in a monastery, and everything else is minor, a mouse in the wall, an old clock striking the wrong time. To come across his cold ear in the warmth of his face and neck was like coming across a shell on the warm beach, it still cold from the sea, and his round neck encircled by her hands was like a Greek column also warmed by a loving sun. These secondary metaphors came edging into Georgiana's imagination from habit and plenty of time as she had had in her past loves, but after a while her love straightened out again and only in his prolonged and final absence did she think of similes and peripheral scenery; and he receding into his back-drop until it was like a picture by Rousseau.

Used to superlatives, this lad's "woman, woman," touched

Georgiana's heart with its wholesome proletarian appeal and her womanhood responded; full grown she accepted his head upon her breast and finally his smiling mouth and his sleep there as well. He taught her, too, that love was fun, he made her laugh between kisses (he was the one), and this amazed and shocked her, love having been solemn for her always, serious, tragic, even, and death the answer if unsatisfactory. In spite of this tragic approach she recognized, nevertheless, that she herself was loved most, or so it appeared, when she was happy, even silly, absurd, giggling like a school girl; not one of her loves, she thought, had loved her when she was sad, emotionally upset, vaporish, grief-stricken; instead of kissing away her tears, which she felt would be very sweet, they had turned away their heads; wanted to be off; were; although artistically, at least, she was at her best at these times; very beautiful for anyone who had the eyes to see it. Well, here then was the lad who made the most of her all her moods, gay or sad, who recognized in the tears a passionate response and who kissed the wet eyes and the wet mouth with equal fervor and happily accepted this sad sympton with equal pleasure.

What chance or star, what flighty hostess, brought these two together when each had served in a way so many others and would continue to do so, I cannot say; and whether they were two positives or two negatives neither can I say. That their proximity was a complete waste, however, in avowals, denials, time and money, I may say without hesitation and like two fires set to cure each other in nothingness and safety, that is what happened, but not before eyelashes were singed and smoke proclaimed their whereabouts. He loved her at once; recognized her highest qualities with the perception of a disappointed lover, a man whose adoration had found no sustained image, whose love had been accepted by a number of women who had loved him but had not appreciated his nature nor taken the trouble to recognize a spiritual quality which they had not sought. They had accepted his love-making and completely satisfied by it had not asked for more. And more is what he wished to give and wished to take. Like a dreamy girl, then, this otherwise experienced lover, or like a resentful woman whose body has been accepted but whose higher tastes have not been inquired into; less talented in love-making he might have discovered those qualities sooner which he respected partly because they eluded him. Georgiana had no way of knowing these things until it was too late. She found her new love difficult to follow, lovable, irritating, untruthful. He was always playing horse, as it were, and in spite of her own propensity to chameleon-like changes according to her daydreams, she was frustrated and annoyed by his. Only once in a while did a bit of himself in the sensible continued story of his existence appear and, "with these scraps," she asked herself, "was she to make out the whole man?" and when she did with a diligence which precluded any other activity "would she want him?" "Listen, silly," she said in annoyance, "who are you today, a famous doctor? Don Quixote? Massine?" He also subjected her to the wanderings of his subconscious, a kind of stream-of-consciousness monologue that he favored as proof that he was uninhibited and her disciplined mind as well as her sensibilities resented it; but she forgave and forgot these psychic gropings of his, although not recognizing them as such, and loved him as he had been loved before, as a male; a beautiful mythological-looking, blue-eyed one, at that, whose delicate, appreciative love-making, as I have said, made her feel all eyes, all mouth, and her daydreams temporarily at a standstill; suspended. It was quite a treat like an ice cream soda after a tennis match. It was her one purely physical attachment and she candidly told him, "You are the only beast in my life," sickening him, making him cry. He resented her quick response to his touch, so unlike herself, and so new her love to herself, that she quite naturally felt that it must be new to him, wasn't he surprised? (No, he wasn't), able as a woman is, even an observing one, to believe that she is the only one, that this is his first love, that everything she does must be new to him as it is to her, a brand new sequence, the end not anticipated and consequently somewhat spoiled as it is to a male who knows what he is about and what he wants and when it is finished. What Georgiana did not realize at first, in her simple-minded innocence, was that this lover hated her. But I have said it too fast. More aware of the inevitable, the inescapable, than she, who was never aware of it at all but conscious only of newness, he could not enjoy the love he felt for her but restlessly attempted to reach for higher plums, pomegranates, he wanted *herself:* her quality, her being; he wanted her conversation; but unwilling to go up stairs one at a time, he *had* to make love to her, he did it so well. Handicapped by his talent, as it were, he could not get her attention. I do not mean that he unwillingly caressed her, giving generously what he believed a woman expected, but it was as if he did not know how to start a conversation with a lioness, he being the lion tamer. Close to him, besides, she took away his voice as well as his words, more as if she were a killing northeast wind than a warm sirocco, and he was doubly speechless. They smiled in a kind of idiocy (not unattractive) at each other and looked into each other's eyes searchingly, seriously, with apprehension, pre-occupied. Then sighing, stretching, yawning, they began to talk, if you can call it that, but it was not exactly conversation.

She: No.
He: Yes.
She: Yes.
He: No.
She: Please.
He: What is it? What is it?
She: Nothing, nothing, nothing. Much.
He: You. You.
She: Your mouth; it.
He: Ah. Ah.
She: Smile, mouth; don't stop.
He: Oh, woman, woman.
She: Ah.

He: Your.
She: No ... No ....
He: What ....
She: Why.
He: Let us look out the window.
She: It might just possibly snow.

In perfect comfort from mouth to knee; each returning, giving, little pressures; each in turn feeling, giving, taking; mutually, intimately moving when most at rest to new scenes, different fields, a like position further on; a separate new joining of mouths; twining of arms; soft elbow pain; swift, hard kneecap meetings, gently away again; warm lifting thighs, then long and taut, shorter and high, sighing, turning, resting but not for long; sweet love; gentle acceptance; generous gifts; pliant lips, eager red mouth, inspired, beaten, subjected, ready and willing again for new shapes, new sounds; pattering noises, rain, wet shining patterns; give and take; give and take; away and come again .... Her head skillfully arranged by him as if it had no interfering body, far enough back on his arm and away from him to give him a start, to let him use his full strength, to make her feel his weight without hurting her or breaking off this dark, warm vessel of a thing, this vase, which is what he would really like to do, and take home with him to play with, he kissed her the way he knew how. When it was going nicely, he would rearrange her, begin again. His mouth fell upon hers like fruit from a tree, warm, bruising itself, wet, shining, dividing itself in two, then four, then eight, and seeming to leave a hollow place which filled up and begged to be hollowed out again. His eager mouth was not ashamed of its own language and she understood it without having heard it before and the little animal sounds soon became a pleasant exciting obbligato which she missed when he kissed her with less abandon, less frank pleasure as if someone were eavesdropping, or as if to make her say, "Please, more sounds," as she finally did, and he, "More noises?" She had received his first kiss with an open mouth but it did not take her long to learn, not before he showed a slight critical impatience, however, that he wanted to separate her lips with his own and this beginning and beginning and beginning, letting him always open a door rather than opening it for him was the first thing he taught her to give him pleasure. Then his tongue like a flame entered her mouth and this strange delight shocked her at first so that she turned her head away and shut her teeth down, tears burning her eyes, ashamed, but of her ignorance and sudden coolness. Patiently he began all over again and gently, sweetly, fondled her lips with his tongue; parted them; went in; stayed awhile, and went away, and again, until at first only in his absence did she recall the pleasure of it and want to have it happen until at last it became a deep, dark pleasure, expected, waited for, encouraged, and in the end a mutual caress; she only daring to go a little way, however; and her explorations were timid, tickled him, made him laugh and anticipate her brave attempts. Finally, in her shyness, she chose his ear and while he only closed his mouth around and breathed warmly into hers, delighting her, she caressed the intricacies of his as if it were a complicated sweet-tasting sea shell, with a pointed tongue like a humming bird, which heretofore had entered only into the literary images of the maze of speech, teasing, it is true, the ears of philosophers, giving them dialectic shivers, no doubt. This delicious lovemaking she accepted as if it were a basket of fruit, or a bouquet; she felt no remorse, no regret, no surprise. She never thought of him anymore when he was gone or dreamed of his coming back; her pleasure in his arms existed all by itself, like a collision. She seemed unaware that her last love was hardly decently out of the room, before she was eagerly accepting the caresses of another. She did feel a certain cold fear in his presence, however, the one before the last; that everlasting, unrequited dark-eyed lover who never really left the premises and to whom she will return; and the feeling that there must be stolen jam on her chin made her fear his searching gaze; but she only felt uneasy for a short while, her deeper psychic feeling returning in his presence improved by the loving words and sweet embrace of her private lover who was like a fulfilled, wishful dream after a trying day, calming her, quieting her, giving her confidence in herself, making her gentler, less impatient with Eric and more desirable to him than ever because she was less desperate, happier, gayer, relieving his feeling of responsibility and desire to be rid of her, loving her so. It was as if, on a hunger strike, she had access to the pantry.

She said to Eric, "You ought to love me because I must indeed be a mystery to you." And again, "I have a horror of pursuing you; you are afraid; I had that insight into you a long time ago and thought I had better not take the initiative but the sad thing about having insight is that it keeps within its own boundaries and is of no practical value. It isn't even logical to *act* upon insight, is it? That is why people who have it are worse off in a practical world than people who haven't; they see what's going to happen but they can't change or stop anything. Awful. And it's people like that who know best the meaning of the word 'inevitable.' A nasty word." The other one would have liked this little conversation but he didn't get it. He got a womanly and passionate response (his own fault), his appeal being such, practiced and smart; while this one wondered at the queer limitations and sideways ways, the biological indifference, almost, of his little sweetheart, who seemed to ask nothing but his constant attention (his own fault).

About here we should, although we are a little ahead of our heroine because she was unconscious of it, notice that she began to be dissatisfied with the lack of integration that she formally had accepted. I suppose she had thought that with something from each she could put the two things together and make one; but they wouldn't superimpose; they remained two as if she were drunk, and as if, after all, mathematics is a stubborn set of symbols. She will later find that her physical love for Michael will make her squirm uneasily in the abstract arms of Eric and vice versa. What a mess; what a prolonged and anxious dream;

what a failure of focus, of her lovers to come out even, of herself
to know what she wanted.

In the meantime: with Michael it was: "Please . . . I am tired . . .
please let us get up . . . please . . . Michael." Exhausted, weary,
cool to him after a long afternoon, evening and early morning of
their lovemaking, Georgiana felt nothing now but the hardness
of his knees, the full weight, doubled by his energy, of his body,
so slim but much too much to carry around like this forever, it
seemed, forever and ever. Only with all her strength had she been
able, with both hands up to his face, to signify to him that she was
through kissing; would he please let go; she was weary, and that
strength, all in her arms, so slight that he could only guess that
she was pushing his face up and away, was failing her at last, and
he also in spite of a single-minded desire to reach her, to claim
her, to find her, which he expressed by his weight and pressure,
his mouth seeming to be digging in the well of hers which was
bottomless, without respite and without conclusion, suspicious
and unhappy one, sensed before it began to fall away the lack of
response, the fatigue, the cooling of her body beneath him. But
not yet angry, still tender, he withdrew his body from hers,
"Up?" gently helped her to a sitting position beside him and
they looked at each other's pale faces, rather than into each
other's eyes, still shining with the desire of the whole day behind
them, not yet showing the discontent of their mouths, which
sulky, mangled, still smiled, nevertheless, in an apologetic way.
In spite of the languor of her whole body Georgiana's brain received from her eyes the fascinating message of observance and
wonder, "His mouth is bright red; his mouth is scarlet; my mouth
that he sees is white . . . white mouth with lavender edges which
was a moment ago scarlet; and his white, whiter than mine now
is, white with the pressure of his feeling for me, a white mouth
with a tragic line between the compressed lips — and a beautiful
swelling just above the upper one as if he would speak, call me
a nice name, make a phrase especially for me. What has happened
that we have exchanged mouths? *'Faites vos jeux,* ladies and

gentlemen, the red or the white.'" And so each gazed at the other's mouth and exchanged something besides kisses. Georgiana heard only a gentle whirring in her ears while she still stared at his whole face rather than into or at his eyes, into or at his mouth, and this either weary or purposeful lack of focus was restful and his face looked like an imperfect print which did not tire her gaze with hard edges and brilliant lights, something she hardly needed to concentrate upon at all, and she didn't. But just at this restful, intermediate split second, it was time for his anger, and taking her hand away from the place along his chest where she had softly placed it to rest it, he threw it away, watched it drop; and turned away from her a fretful, stubborn, angry look and presented it to the ashes in the fireplace, as it were, the warm powdery grey of their density interspersed and dotted with innumerable cigarette butts of his own smoking, his own discontent, his own savage ways. (And she so well brought up by grandpère! What contempt the old man would have felt for this one: confounded impudence!)

"Are you passing the time of day?" he said, petulantly, bitterly, rhetorically. She could not be angry, she was too tired. She looked at the heroic white neck leading out of his shirt, a white column which she felt between her two hands which lay in her lap making no effort to clasp the actuality but arching as if they did. Her eyes closed but no warm darkness came, only streaks, brilliant, white, sputtering lines, and the noise in her ears increased; she tried to think about something but what? "Pass the time, pass the time, pass the time, please . . . of day." She worked very hard and lifted the lids up and over her rounded eyeballs and then with an effort projected her look as far as him: his face in his hands, his long fingers bisecting, trisecting, five-secting it, he must be weeping. He lifted his head immediately and he was; he stared gloomily at her. With all her strength, the only feeling for him that had not been tapped, despoiled, completely used up this day, came to her assistance: her maternal instinct; that instinct, when the object is a full grown man, which can only be called in quantity and quality a puny passion; that in-between feeling went out to this crybaby, this angry, frustrated, little boy, this motherless, blue-eyed little bastard, who wanted to be rescued metaphorically from the roof, it seemed, and with some feeling she cried, "Baby. Poor little thing."

"I am not a baby. I am not a poor — a little — or a thing — I am not a thing."

"Mmmmmmm, Baby."

Stretching out his long legs, lifting his chin, he placed his heavy head upon her breast, sighed, and giving up to her keeping, everything: his body, his soul, his ambition, his sorrows and joys as if she were a cupboard and also in charge of the key, he immediately went to sleep, without affectation, or was it? "Innocent," she thought, "irresponsible, leaving everything to me as usual," and she let her chin sink upon his hair slowly not to waken him and finally she felt his hard skull, and she shut her teeth down upon each other until as time passed they began to ache, and the weight of his whole body once more but without intent, desire, direction, sank upon hers and his warm flesh without outline or edges, without bones, it seemed, was like a coverlet and she, all alone, without his consciousness, began to recall long-ago nightmares, the weight in one's heels, the household cat upon one's chest, the oppressive stillness and sick pressure of a summer night, the thick breasts of her ancient mammy, her purple breath and rich endearments, the nightmare of too many covers with questionable subject matter, the feeling of safety pins the only safeguard of her explosive lungs as she sought the surface of a childhood lake.

"GRAND-PÈRE!"

And she woke herself with the name of the old man ricocheting back to her ears from the corners of the room and a desperate fear in her mind, her heart racing, her skin stinging, and at last, relief, gratitude, to find only a blond head upon her chest and sweet daylight in the room, the mauve of its tone turning her lover's hair green. Unconscious of the nightmare significance of her cry, reassured, but feeling for a little while that she was in the center of her childhood, her dream, whatever it had been, still with her, her conscious mind found an immediate answer in the circumstantial evidence of her blue-eyed lover, her little cousin, and she accepted the wrong answer. A tag-end confusion began in her mind, however, and she felt dissatisfied and uneasy. She willed her heart to be quiet for fear of its beat in his ear but he was awake and in a humble mood; no longer a little boy he turned down her blouse and kissed her softly three times between her breasts.

"I was asleep?"

"Yes, for a long time."

"Thank you," he said politely and lightly as if for a cigarette, and raising himself, standing, he removed a bent one from a rumpled package, lit it, pulled it from his mouth, bowed slightly from the hips with real grace like a dancer, took a step sideways toward the door, bowed again, a smile curving his lips but his whole demeanor, — another step, — gently sarcastic, teasing, "Thank you." A thin pain attached itself to her finger tips at his graceful independent departure, his slight sneer. His beauty held her attention but she felt unloved, suspended in mid-air, quite momentarily lost. Did he love her? Fear was her answer, a white streak from breast to breast and down her sides. He was watching. She was brave, rather bright, did not ask about the next meeting but wondered desperately if there was to be one. "Goodbye, Michael, dear."

"Michael, the avenging angel," he still smiled, without happiness in his look, however.

"Michael, the pugilistic angel," she said, feeling a little better, but not wanting to hurt him and "When," she asked almost timidly but not quite, "When?"

"Oh, sometime." He tossed it off, watching her, moving away, prancing a little, enjoying, it appeared, his sudden independence and her lack of it, nasty thing. She felt there was no use and did not ask again. "Oh, all right." She was near tears; did not like the position she was in; felt no anger, wished she could; in quick defeat pleaded, "Tuesday?"

"That depends." (Was he grinning?)

"Dog!" (Sadly.)

"Thank you." (Lightly.)

"Oh." (In real annoyance.)

And his leaving her like this made her unhappy again; and she could not remember the happiness he had taught her for the cruelty of his teasing, the knifelike pain of his sarcasm; his will-o-the-wisp pretense left her with the feeling that he had been playing when he was in fact serious, that he not only did not love her but actually disliked her. This brought a quick moan to her lips followed by anger but so slight an anger that it did not purify itself and the residue kept her busily discontented, irritable, expressed by symbolic denials (shaking her head, kicking the furniture), and a lack of concentration on anything outside her problem with Michael. The fact that he was a problem was his only intellectual benefit to Georgiana, or should I say drawback? Georgiana learned that there is only one complete anesthesia: physical love; but that it leaves one intellectually jumpy. How could her dreams run smoothly with this strange lover who seemed to want to leave her each time with an asp in her breast, in the very place he so gently but ardently kissed. The pain of his unkindness erased the memory of his tender intense love-making and the genuine misery of his unfulfilled desires, giving his love a truthfulness not to be denied; and she was not happy in his absence, only in his presence; in fact she forgot him, as I have said; this being exactly the opposite behavior of her love for the other one whom she loved more deeply in his absence than in his presence; and whom she always went to meet in her imagination, anticipating his coming and following him in her thoughts after he had gone (she watched him in her mind's eye turning the corners toward home, going up the steps, greeting the cat, putting out the lights; to bed) filling up pleasantly the interim of his absences.

She began to reflect upon this: and she became conscious that in Michael's absences she wanted Eric and so she returned to him. She took her time about it; gave herself the very dear pleasure of it in her imagination and then took the initiative as usual with him, telephoned him, said fearfully, "Hello, Eric, I miss you," and felt her heart beat hard with excitement waiting for his "Yes, I will come" and no faithlessness to Michael at all which made her want to skip, light-hearted, when she heard Eric's step upon the stairs; standing still went to meet him, saw his dark, warm face and felt his smooth hands before he appeared in the room, "How does he project himself like that, is he a ghost?" But in his actual presence, she felt a quick icy fear as if caught in a lie and no exit. His eyes searched into hers. Before she had time to think that perhaps it was unwise she was on her knees, her head in his lap, sobbing, tossing her head, clenching her fists, quite a sight, deeply and profoundly unhappy without subject matter, it appeared, to her misery. How she remembered this one! A sentimental nostalgia mounted to her brain. He did not stir; said nothing. She did everything, as usual; pulled his handkerchief out of his pocket; kissed his knees that were wet with her tears; finally pulled herself together, took his hand and arching his fingers for him placed it on her head. He began to stroke her hair evenly, but with a slight muscular tremor at the end of each stroke that she liked very much and she shut her stinging eyes and quieted down; felt quite good, began to explain, anticipating his questions which she knew he would ask. It went something like this:

"When you are in love," she said, "it must show on your face."

"Yes?"

"In your eyes, I think."

"Yes?"

"And maybe other people see it."

"Perhaps."

"Do you think so?"

"It may be."

"And so I think it is appealing to someone."

"Do you?"



"Yes, I think perhaps a person sees love in your eyes — in your look, your manner, and he likes it — maybe you are very attractive and look as if you wanted him, do you think so?"

"You tell me."

"Of course it isn't him."

"No. Tell me."

"Oh, I am just thinking and wondering and I think maybe it is really so."

"Why did you cry?"

"I am unhappy."

"Yes."

"Not really."

"No."

"But don't you really think what I say is really true?"

"Is it anyone I know?"

"It isn't anyone — what I think is that I love you so much and have for so long and people see it; perhaps it shows. It must show, don't you think?"

"How long ago was it, this one?"

"Oh a long time, a long time ago."

She began to tell the truth out of context. It went like this: "You don't know him at all, you never saw him," she picked out Serge who four years previously she had met at a party and their flirtation for all to see had been described as "Terrific." This part she did not tell, but she began to talk of him, to describe him, to tell how he had seen her and fallen in love with her; it was true, she was telling the truth; she forgot Michael completely and recalled the passionate face and gestures of another one, the one who made love to her so unhesitatingly, but whom she loved only at first glance and never again, a nuisance, a passionate lover in a hurry who had not known how to treat her, nor she him, and so it ended at once, with a crash, as it were, and she had put it aside, forgotten it purposely because she had played, she felt, an unfortunate role. It had been messy, a vulgar flirtation on her part, not a bit nice, but she drew it out now when it was needed and it became the story of Michael but with an understudy. She began to feel better and better as she told the truth about someone else and she did not feel at all that she was lying, probably because she was not. Not only was everything she said true in detail and sequence but aside from the actual identity of the person involved, the problem was the same and of what importance is a name? Michael, Arthur, John, perhaps; as a matter of fact, it was delicacy on her part, who knows, to leave his name out of it, and besides she named him Michael herself, he was no real Michael at all. In any event, a sweet, dishonest, foggy calm crept over her and she even felt as she said, "Is it clear?" that it was.

Relieved because he wanted to be relieved he said, "Do you feel better?" and felt better himself.

Georgiana had sharp eyes, noted his jealousy and uneasiness as she talked and his relief when it turned out to be someone he did not know rather than someone else whom he had immediately suspected, the one who was real and whose bright red past and seductive charm he knew. And so anxious was he to deny any attachment between these two, that he believed her histrionic tale, and being by training a realistic person, only the actual man, of his own knowledge, someone he could lay his hand on and call by name could be his rival, so that Georgiana might give in amorous detail the story of another's love, if he did not know him and especially if it was yesterday, he did not have to believe in his existence; he was to all intents and purposes non-existent; a tree falling in the forest and no one to hear could not be "Timber" to him, could it? Unconsciously Georgiana wanted to stir him and consequently, although she had cleverly relieved herself of a confession that would do, she felt disappointment at the ease with which he maneuvered his feelings so that they would come out even; she wanted a fifth act, or at least an epilogue, but hesitated to arouse this man she loved so much and whose vital anger she did not wish turned upon her and so she contented herself with the thought, "Another time," and began now to concentrate on him. She wrapped her arms around his legs lowering her head to hide her eyes, and felt his knees press into her breasts. A sharp pain sped down her body, lingering an instant too long, causing her to make a short musical wail as she let out the breath that she had taken in with the beginning of her sigh at his nearness, the smell of him, his blackness, the fatal, everlasting, incestuous remembrance of an old picture, a dark head, a warm fear. Quickly it was gone, all of it, and in tenderness she kissed the insides of both his hands, so soft, warm in the center, cool at the tips, the cushioned pulsating ends as full and more responsive than his lips which was lucky as he seldom allowed her to kiss him on his mouth. And so she pleasantly, happily, started all over again, let the tenderness pass as the end of a sequence in her feelings and began again to revive her pleasure, seeking again the pain. He let her wet his fingers with her tongue and kiss them quickly, in her pretense, her desire for his mouth, but with no need to close her eyes for fear of his gaze, and the wish to be by herself with no interruption — shy — she retired by herself, into herself, in her love-making and this finger-kissing with lowered head delighted her and lasted a long time. Finally, feeling, sensing her concentration, afraid of it, wanting to protect her from something, he drew away his hand, interrupting her, but not before she had quickly nibbled his middle finger leaving her teeth prints and raising a small mound of flesh brightened with her lipstick.

"You hurt me."

"You hurt *me*."

She knew from long experience with him that he was scared; gave him time for composure before she again took his hands, stroked them with the tip of a forefinger.

"Voltaire said that dark skin was softer than fair," she said, "but I knew it first."

"You're funny."

Eric wrapped his fingers around her wrist; she felt happy, receptive, waited. Suddenly she lifted her head, sat motionless; she had noticed a faint but positive smell of fresh paint. "Nothing has been painted here," she said to herself. He began gently to caress her palm. "Soft, warm, damp, clinging, exciting, lovely," the words sped through her mind. "Mister Moon!" Dropping her head upon his knee she began to tremble.

"What is it?"

"Oh I love you, I love you so. I cannot bear it."

"Never mind."

She looked at him. Not really minding the sharp, slick memory of Mister Moon, she eagerly stared at the beloved face of her favorite, the one with whom she felt so safe, so secure, but at the same time so passionately, dangerously, attached to, and recognizing once more over and over again a faded, but nevertheless brilliant, retouched photograph, a dark head, a thrilling contour — a kind of innocent voluntary incest, an exciting spiritual affiliation held her in its spell and she was as happy for the moment as she would ever be. Rising with him as he was about to leave, linking her arm affectionately in his for the short walk to the stairway not to miss a bit of him, she watched absentmindedly their two pairs of feet keeping step, hers in soft kid with a strap across the instep, his in fine sole leather, shiny, and toeing, a little bit, out. ("Everyone does when he is older." Does what?) She disengaged her arm; refused to accept the memory, fought with it, snubbed it; and learned nothing in consequence from this queer state of receptivity that she was momentarily in, because that is not what she wanted, I suppose.

"Goodbye."

"What is the matter?"

"Nothing."

"Well, goodbye."

"Goodbye; it really is — nothing."

"Goodbye."

"Goodbye."

Following him to the door and finding the outside air brilliant, cold, and a big moon, besides, she felt strong again and went a little way with him. Both began to shiver, a combination of past emotion and a change of temperature, and Georgiana hung on to Eric, arching her neck to watch his profile. What was the matter? How cruel! In the moonlight the beloved, dark, warm face with clear soft edges that looked so much like her own handwriting appeared peaked, shrunken. A pinched profile lay along her own; the snow looked like linen behind it, a little blue. A stubborn little face with outthrust chin marched beside her. She was overcome with pity, remorse; horror.

No! No!

Used to her changes of mood, and her sensitivity to changes in temperature, he took her home, placed his warm lips on her cold ones to reassure her, which it didn't, shoved her inside, and left her.

She began, in her unhappiness, finally, to pick a quarrel with him, and she noticed that he, too, in this instance, appeared unconsciously to be doing the same thing. This was the result, in ordinary circumstance, it might appear, of their platonic but constantly anticipatory love: the imminent quarrel was perhaps a desire for action, a desire by two willful people to get something over with, to rid themselves decisively of each other; end it; each loving each to the point where freedom from each other became a survival reversion, self-preservation, a desire for the other's removal, even by death. What a relief to be rid of one's love: how nice to walk alone, and she remembered the everlasting vacation she had had from the little cousin that she had loved the most. What a happy ending: death to love; what a fair exchange is no robbery. But wasn't there more to it than this, enough as it was? What was the cause of grandpère, long since dead, coming back like this and interfering with her love life if you wanted to call it that? Just when she was happiest, at least about to be content, it seemed, in walked grandpère. Was he jealous of her, too, as he had been of the aunts, posthumous patriarch, p.s. to his earthly dictatorship, just one more fling at running things? Not exactly. This isn't a ghost story. But Georgiana was afraid just as much as if it was. After a week or two of grandpère haunting the premises Georgiana said to herself clearly, "Michael reminds me of my little cousin who is dead and Eric of my father who doesn't exist. I wish Michael was dead not Eric. That's something but there is a lot more to do and why grandpère? I was trying to solve grandpère's reappearance and I solved something else." She never did solve grandpère's unexpected returns, uninvited old guest, though she successfully figured that her physical attachment to Michael was an encore somehow of her games with the blue-eyed cousin, *bis!* while her more spiritual and unrequited love for Eric was *in memoriam*, as it were, to her invisible, disembodied, unincarnate father; a kind of hallowed passion. Making love to the latter (Eric) was exciting, everlasting, safe. Hadn't the gay, red bull mystically promised her to stay in his pen? Hadn't grandpère (why grandpère?) arranged it for her? How wonderful and without the growing quarrels, more and more frequent, would be her and his love if they were one in thought and he had comprehended, and better still if she had! Her conclusions remained inconclusive; her logic (perfectly correct), her deductions (circumstantial), did not give her the peace they should have. Her simplifications made her more restless instead of quieter. These simplifications, grown up as she was, at least in frame, inches, time, were a part of her psychic character, unable to change: as a child, without realizing it, because she was determined to love and admire her dark father, she made her mother whom we have not mentioned because she didn't, blue-eyed, photographs, paintings and hearsay to the contrary; denied her; feeling the distinctness of persons as she did, antagonism for those on the other side, the blue-eyed side. (She, too, had a Bible in her mind, like grandpère's real one, with names crossed out.) She felt that her mother must have been on the wrong side, beloved as she had been to idolatry by grandpère who was on the wrong side and mistreated, it seemed to grandpère, by the lovely wicked one, her father. The fact that her mother might have been as dark-eyed, as uneven as herself, she never imagined because how could she separate the loved from the unloved? Answer: she chose to do so by coloration. Some of her antagonisms, attractions, are discovered to be arbitrary, therefore, because in this way things come out even, problems are solved, things fit, man is rational, Georgiana can sleep. And so her division of blue and brown was sensible: "He who is not for me is against me." She explained the cousin as a variable, blue-eyed but the best of the lot, infant propinquity; and Mister Moon as an exaggeration. How dark he was! And what a reckless color scheme was hers! Laying aside the problem as intellectually solved she began to use up the energy that was left in a parallelism of physical action. The idea being, I suppose, to get it over with on both fronts at once. The trouble was: she did not in her physical behavior have any idea of what she was doing; it seemed to manage by itself; and her instigation of a full program of quarrels with both lovers was intuitive and painful. She began to quarrel systematically but cleverly so that no one ever knew who was doing the quarreling. She deliberately, it seemed, made herself unloved, but held her ground as a female should, allowing her lovers to leave *her*, as is proper in life and in literature, including the Scandinavian.

She quarrelled faster and more definitively with Michael than with Eric; it was easier, more exciting, even rewarding, because she seemed to hate him convincingly, thinking him merely a variable. It wasn't so hard or penetrating, so like slow torture as severing herself from Eric, plucking out an eye, cutting off an arm. She wished he was dead (Michael). She fought with him by mail, by telephone, and in his arms. Her kisses were bites, her surrenders contempt. He thought he was leaving her and in a way he was. The little flag he thought he had seen over her cabin "Owner aboard" had changed its colors, its design, its meaning, and he was disappointed. Attracting him as she had by her spiritual possibilities, his prowess had made her change her mind, if it can be called that, and she had jumped overboard to continue the metaphor with a very pleasurable fish. But the fish had sighed for wings and been denied them. He got only what he seemed to want which he did not want but despised. So you see, it wasn't very hard to break with Michael. She nevertheless did a good job of it, didn't deny him his deserts, didn't short change him. But being a woman, as I have said, no double-sexed snail, as it were, she let her lovers leave the premises without a *coup de grâce*, and she felt a certain dissatisfaction, a sexual defeat because that is the way things are. She never could bring herself to strike the final blow, to annihilate the male. After a long spell of quarreling, she recognized that it was a blow-by-blow victory, I suppose, that there was no need logically of a knockout, but as time went on and doors closed behind her lovers, leaving her moody and introspective, she felt that the male was still at large, innocent, the silly thing, of his defeat, roaming around with hydrophobia, and she unable, because of her sex, to sock it to him. "Eels all come from, and eventually return to, the Saragossa Sea," she said when she found both Michael and Eric irretrievable, but she didn't know exactly what she meant. Do you?

And it didn't happen so fast: it required patience to get rid of Eric whom she loved as best she could, with all her heart and intelligence; she had to be patient with him and with herself to lose him. Their accordion-like affection was not as quick to take offense as the absurd muscular affair with the blue-eyed bastard and there were more aches and pains to it than the localized misery of Michael's withdrawal, a negative female pain at most. She suffered from that awful feeling, when quarrels are in the semi-finals, that only the disappearing object is desirable, only the lost cannot be found and that nothing else will do. It's like going through a lost-and-found list: he is not there; nothing is eligible; this is the end; there he goes. But like a cat it happened to her more than once and from her high place from which she could not get down she got a cat's-eye view of her own anxiety. No one ever rescued her, either; she finally came down herself, but backwards, and accepted skimmed milk. In her anger at this dual defeat, this double feature she was sitting through, she couldn't help, in the intermissions, her weaker moments, suddenly left by herself, returning to Eric, but never to Michael. The latter she kept after, however, not so much to hold his attention a little longer as to be sure he was finished, *fini*, that his hold on her was broken. She insulted him in letters and over the telephone. She made a lot of little feminine epigrams that he ought to have had embroidered on his shirt front: "You're quite nice but impossible." "It's easy to be fond of you but hard to excuse you." "Women don't really like cruelty, they just put up with it." "You are so blind that a dog could not help you, can a dog lead a dog?" "You are so vain that you think women are cute who insult you." And in a note, "Did you think you could make a friend of me so easily? Without even trying? Just charm me into it? I told you what it was that friendship was based on, but you got tired before you had built the foundation and in digging a hole you lost sight of the sky, and there never was a cornerstone and if there had been I can just see what would have been in it! pieces of your old loves (loves!), hair-ribbons, fingernails, pearly teeth, dimples, tears, too, love letters and telephone numbers. Bastard! You thought because of a natural easy attraction and intimacy that you could speak to me familiarly. You are not entitled to any such intimacy. Don't you dare use words to me: words can wait." And again ". . . this quarreling disgusts me. I hate to think we know each other well enough to quarrel but at least as we do, damn it, I wish I were a female spider; then I could have shut my eyes and gulped you down, satisfying my horrid appetite but never having to face you again without my innocence." This innocence which Georgiana really seemed to possess and which she knew she possessed as if she were Diana with a renewable maidenhead or Marcia, *vierge perpétuelle*, frustrated both these lovers, one in possession though he was, equally. It was a kind of mind over matter innocence that she exercised, refusing ever to be fooled into the facts of life; a kind of voluntary blindness. I need not say it had its charm, but it irritated both men and each wished to seduce her

with any weapon she cared to name; she closed her eyes and ears
to sword and word alike.

Michael: "You have had plenty of experience."

Georgiana: "Experience is something you notice, my love."

And the other one, so subtle, appealing in a queer unapproach-
able way, himself; with a pigeon-holed kind of innocence of his
own, deliberately, one evening, instead of choosing a dreamy
setting for their pleasures, annoyed, as he was at her romantic
approach, wishing to seduce her mind, as it were, her preference,
took her to a strange place where he must have been before and
which must have come to mean physical reality to him, the
seamy side of love: what appeared at first to be a beautiful
promontory surrounded by a quiet sea, topped by an especially
gentle greenish moon, turned out to be a rotting pier frequented
by homeless lovers with keen appetites and no fuss about it; in
its shadows, gin bottles and rats; above the sound of waves,
hoarse voices and vulgar camaraderie, hushed only, at moments,
by the rhythmic approach of a big cop who like Georgiana kept
his eyes on the moon; neither saw or heard a thing, but Georgiana's heart beat fast as if she were in danger. A decade at least
too late she learned that innocence is hated by man who lost his
own so long ago in a very pretty garden, and being without it,
angry at his loss, he cannot help the wish to de-flower those
whom he suspects of possessing it, and until he succeeds in this
kind of brotherhood of man, this democratic state, he is frustrated and irritable, especially if he is willful. And the scene
came back to her of grandpère when she inadvertently surprised
him with his pants down (without even a piece of greenery!
poor man) that time when she was not so much innocent as
ignorant. How he sat on the edge of his bed in his shirt, pantless,
holding what she guessed might be an early Christmas present,
and how he must have ground his hind teeth in anger at this
allegory of innocence, which stared at him so steadily; herself.
She saw, now, what the old man had hated: not her, but what
she represented. Imagine Adam's irritation if Eve had not fallen,

too! If after *her* bite she had remained as clear-eyed as ever, "Why, what's the *matter*, Adam?" Wouldn't he have spent the rest of his days trying to persuade the first convert: to sin? An apple a day?

But it was not easy, as I have said, to quarrel with Eric. She tried to shock him but quickly quit because she couldn't bear to change the picture of herself in his imagination, the one she hoped he had. She tried the epigrammatic, smart-alecky, un-womanly approach, but he thought she was just plain funny and laughed and laughed. This put her off her intention: she loved to make him laugh. She felt she was very close to him when they were funnily eye-to-eye; as if nerve endings were pinned together; as if she were giving him her blood, arm to arm. "When a person laughs at your jokes," she thought, "he is yours for the moment, body and soul, and as nude as a peeled willow branch." Two weeks of ticklish adoration followed during which she was at her best and he kept stepping aside, cleverly avoiding the thing he loved, she knowing ahead of time which way he would turn and meeting him, right there, but never colliding. What a pleasant game it was, taming a colt who would never be tamed. Something always-and-always to do. Playing with fire? No, just keeping adorably warm. But it was the last ride together. Exhausted as she was by both of them, close to subconscious truths but not close enough to lose consciousness, she began to cry. She did not collapse: was not one of those fortunate ones with amnesia at his finger tips, *petit-mal* to soothe him, even an anxiety-neurosis to scare him out of his wits, migraine so painful as to induce forgetfulness, and during which attacks the mind quickly empties itself, automatic protection, giving itself a rest — her weariness merely made her hypersensitive, subject to tears. No sudden wit's-end relief, just tears, that inbetween relaxation set in. And that did it. She cried all over him; she got him soaking wet; it's a wonder he didn't catch cold. (Who said, "The luxury of dolour?") She couldn't have thought of a quicker way to get rid of him, in fact she hadn't, it wasn't exactly an idea. This one

never had appreciated the salt taste of tears on his mouth, neither
did he harbor the physical cruelty of Michael in his make-up
who had liked the emotional mutual exhibitionism of tears, the
fitful pleasure of scenes. Eric just plain couldn't take it. It made
him feel a general, all-over unlocalized remorse, like the grippe.
It made him see in himself the guilty male. It made him feel
disgust, not of her, which he might have been able to bear, but
of himself. He felt the need to forget something, put it out of
his mind. He couldn't stand the continuous result, *le vilan*,
somehow, of some action of his own, some memory of some
action, he didn't know what; he didn't have time to figure it out,
he just felt it, hated it, fled. Watching him put on his hat and
coat, pack his suitcase, as it were, she got an insight and spoke
straight from it, intuitively. "You're a killer!" "What!" "Oh no!
I'm sorry." But what she meant, if she had analyzed it, was in a
word: What a man wants most is peace and quiet and he will
kill to get it. Terrified of what his emotions will do to his conscious self, recalling the act of love, he hates pandemonium, his
own loss of control. What he hates most, then, is *love*, and all
commotion, even traffic jams, reminds him of it. Yes, he will kill.
"Poor darling," sensing his fright she kissed him, the worst possible thing she could have done. He got up, actually did put on
his hat and coat, really and truly left the premises. He took to
his heels (her little dark Mercury), he fled from it, from her,
from commotion, the loss of free will; a colt, too, but with
God's own brand on his flank, a halo over his ears. (The darling.
Well, goodbye.)

Finality laid its cold hand upon her. She stood alone, independent, free. But free from what? That she did not know and,
not knowing, began to look for it again; started that traditional
ballet all over again. The search for grandpère was unconscious,
so unconscious that I believe if she had been hypnotized she
would have said, "I want my father," and the hypnotist, pleased
with the "right" answer, would have thought, "Of course, how
simple, wonderful thing hypnotism." But deeper in the annals of

uncharted thought, unwanted but willful, grandpère walked in pointed shoes, little beard thrust out, (archaic) with cold blue eyes disproving, if nothing else, the Mendelian color theory. She will continue the search forever in her own short foreverness, fighting grandpère tooth and nail when she finds him, but loving no one who does not resemble him. (*Cherchez grandpère.* [The little man who wasn't there]). Arbitrarily but with some insight, not enough, plenty of logic but an incoherent premise, Georgiana, as I have said, solved her love problem, but not quite. Recognizing both a psychic truth and physical resemblance she thought she saw in Eric and Michael, consequently loving them, but guiltily, her father in the first and her dear blue-eyed boy cousin in the second. This was correct as far as she went but she didn't go far enough. Discovering something, she neglected to discover more. How easily the frail mind of man is satisfied. How he suffers until it is, and how he suffers but philosophically when it finally isn't. Continuing to behave exactly as he did before he discovered the "truth," so did Georgiana, without quite the extra brain, perhaps energy, to see that when a disease is cured so are the symptoms. And so her triumph was an ornamental one, to what I believe is called the ego. Her unhappiness continued. Her love affairs multiplied but without Q.E.D. She never lost her charm, that especial charm of the curious, the hopeful, the steadfast, the polygamous; she "flourished" like a gerund; *desideratum;* was never grotesque, ignoble; chose more and more unrequited love as if, intuitively, she was safe as long as she did not hate herself. But the insufficient answer disproved her conclusions even to herself. Something, she knew, was wrong. For instance, having decided that Michael was the prototype of her cousin she said to herself, "Yes, but maybe the wrong cousin; the cousin allergic to strawberries; the crybaby; mama's boy; little bully; decidedly what I have called Michael in my anger, bastard." And Mister Moon, where did he come from? A dark-skinned, soft to the touch, retroactive variable? Was he the son of ... the son of ... the son of ..., dear reader, Mammy? Why did she so successfully censor the person but not the deed? Didn't she pursue dark men all her life? Was Mammy a deeper, profounder fear, a more overwhelming sexual guilt, than grandpère? Not incestuous, so what? Congo Lesbian? How silly! Black? Evil? Guilt itself? White milk from black breasts, ambivalence then? Intellectual and physical frustration? In desperation she tried to make things come out even. She found, for instance, an answer, one of those simple ones in her fatigue, to her inevitable quarrels; "My cousin is dead, my father is dead: lovers must die." Not bad but not good. Take it away.

To continue our search for the truth much as Georgiana did, in whom, I take it, we are interested, Eric really did resemble the glowing, still warm picture of Georgiana's father in fact, as well as in her imagination because she wanted it like that. But he also resembled, especially as he grew older, especially in his character, her willful, handy-headed grandfather. This cannot be considered an arbitrary coincidence if we will remember that characters in a book are descended from previous ones; totemic, they do not spring full-blown from an author's brow; and if this were the story of Georgiana's father and mother, we would find, perhaps, that Georgiana's mother loved Georgiana's father because he resembled her father, grandpère to Georgiana. O.K.? Not quite. The problem is still there but at least it gathers momentum, as it were, moss, test-tube tradition. Georgiana had heard much of grandpère's attachment to her mother from the aunts, jealous and sometimes sarcastic, and as a very little girl had thought that his cruelty to her was due to the unfortunate fact in her mind, encouraged we must admit by grandpère's actions, that her mother was good (blue-eyed) and she bad (dark-eyed) like her father. (Remember her placing her mother on the blue-eyed list?) When in effect the old man's impatience, irritability, amounting, it is true, to overt acts against Georgiana might have been the result of her resemblance to his little daughter, taken away from him in her sensuous prime by his rival, Georgiana's father, dead in childbirth too, murder! (Not his, thank God!) And here stood Georgiana, a niggardly duplicate, not enough but too much, more than he could bear, a constant reminder, perhaps, of his incestuous bothersome passion for a little girl, a dead one.

Here we are, dear reader, on the spot, with Georgiana; getting so far and no further; wondering if somewhere there isn't an answer, the correct one, on a folded slip of paper or maybe in a cornerstone, or on the back page, printed upside down, of the *Chicago Tribune;* because we feel sure that the only questions God asks are the ones he knows the answers to. As for the author (myself), I submit the following diagram but not as an answer, merely as a symbolic representation of an abstraction:

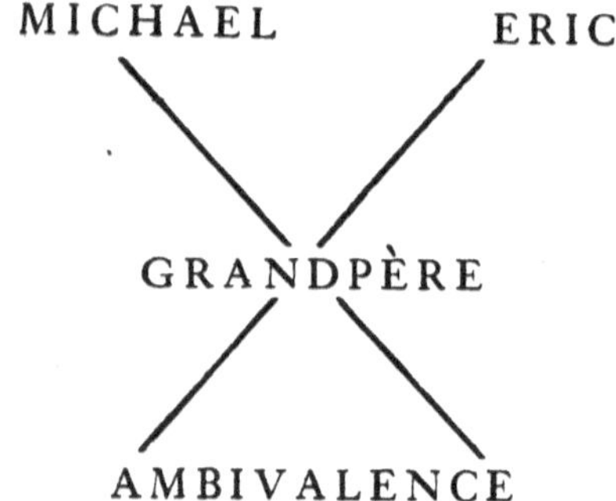


Georgiana, they told me, lay on her death bed as fresh as a daisy; as if she were looking forward to another love affiair; planning its sequences; a little frown on her brow but with red lips, a curving smile. Holding the hand of her lover, a dark-eyed one, unrequited (he, too, seemed unremorseful, almost happy in his brotherly grief), she said things that I suppose were her last words; as uninhibited as words can be as death anesthetizes the conscious intellect, but dramatic, the sense of drama never deserting her speech, saving her from gibberish, from ignominy, in her last moments. "Grandpère," she said very clearly, accepting her lover's warm kiss, "I want to live in a little house with you where nothing squeaks."